The Secret Life of Steffie Martin

by Lurlene McDaniel

Cover photo by Bichsel Morris
Photographic Illustrators

Published by Willowisp Press, Inc.
401 E. Wilson Bridge Road, Worthington, Ohio 43085

Printed in the United States of America

10 9 8 7 6 5 4 3 2 1

ISBN 0-87406-046-X

One

BOXES. Everywhere Steffanie Martin looked in the tiny upstairs bedroom, she saw boxes piled on top of boxes. The movers had stacked them, randomly shoving them into corners as they had unloaded the contents of the moving van into the old two-story white frame house. In her bedroom, they had heaped boxes on her dresser. Or they had left them perched on the bare mattress and box springs in the middle of her bed. They were brown moving boxes . . . old cardboard rejects from the grocery store . . . former containers for paper towels, dishwasher detergent, cereal, and canned goods.

Steffie let out a deep sigh. She threaded her way carefully through the maze of boxes. She opened a curtainless window, allowing the humid, hot August air to invade the room. The tap-tap sound of someone bouncing a ball resounded off the walls. The sound echoed a rhythmic loneliness that reverberated inside Steffie's head.

"Well, what do you think?"

Steffie turned at the question, encountering the blue-eyed gaze of her mother.

"It's all right."

"Just all right?" Alice Martin asked. "I think it's terrific! After all these years of living in apartments, we finally have a whole house that's our own!"

Steffie shrugged. A whole house—but only after another move to another town to another job for her father. Once again, a different school, different friends, a different town. Where was she anyway? Oh, yes. Indiana, she thought to herself.

"A whole house!" Her mother reemphasized. "Imagine. Three bedrooms . . . one for us, one for you. I'll make the third one a sewing room." Mrs. Martin narrowed her eyes at Steffie. "I thought you'd be happier about it than this."

Steffie heard the note of irritation in her mother's voice. "Can I paint my walls lavender?" she asked. That was something she'd never been able to do in the apartments they'd lived in through the years. Landlords didn't like walls painted lavender or purple

4

or bright colors like yellow or orange.

"It's our house. Paint them any color you like," her mom said.

Our house. How many times during the past ten years had I wanted to hear those words? she thought. When she'd been very small it hadn't mattered that her family had moved every six months. But when she started school, it started to matter. Now that she was 14 and entering ninth grade in four weeks, it mattered a lot. She was tired of moving, and tired of pulling up roots and taking off. Often there had been no explanation and little time to prepare.

"Dad's gone to the auto lot to check in with his new boss. On his way home, he'll stop off at a fried chicken place and bring home dinner. How does that sound?" her mother asked.

"I like fried chicken. It's okay by me," Steffie muttered.

"Look, Steffie," her mother said, reaching out and smoothing her daughter's hair, "why don't you go outside for a while and look around? It's a pretty neighborhood. Maybe you'll meet a neighbor."

"I need to get things put away."

"Tomorrow's soon enough, or later tonight. Go on outside."

Secretly, Steffie was relieved to get outdoors. Unpacking always depressed her. She left through the screen door in the rambling kitchen that was piled high with partially unpacked boxes. The door slammed and she bounded down the back porch steps into the sweet, hot air.

The lawn sloped upward toward a white fence with boards missing. An enormous walnut tree rose from the center of the yard. "Great tree!" she said aloud. She calculated the fastest way to climb it. The tap-tap sound of the bouncing ball stopped, leaving only the swishing splat of a lawn sprinkler to fill the void.

"Hey! Can you give me a hand?"

Steffie whirled toward the voice that had called out to her. From the next yard, a boy about her age grinned at her. He was taller than she, which surprised her since she was over five foot six inches. He had thick black hair and big brown eyes that caught the slanting rays of the sun.

"What's the problem?" she asked, feeling suddenly self-conscious in his presence.

"My basketball got hung up in a tree."

"You can't get it down?" Steffie was dubious. He looked muscular and athletic enough to shinny up any tree.

"Not yet." He grinned and tapped his left leg. Curious, Steffie walked over to the low picket fence that separated their yards and looked down. The boy wore blue shorts, but his leg was encased in a plaster cast from his ankle to his thigh.

"How'd you do that?" The question blurted out of her mouth.

"On my dirt bike, six weeks ago. I'm supposed to get it off in a couple of more weeks. I'm counting the minutes." He grinned.

Steffie came around the edge of the fence and eyed the cast. It was dingy and gray with wear. It was covered with inked names and felt-tip drawings. "Where's the tree?" she asked.

"The basketball hoop is around the side, over the garage. The tree's next to it."

Steffie followed him, watching as he hobbled along in the cumbersome cast. He pointed up and she saw the ball wedged between two limbs. "Can you reach it?" he called as she grabbed the tree's massive trunk and swung into the lower branches.

"Got it!" Steffie poked the ball and it fell neatly downward onto the concrete driveway below. The boy retrieved it and fired off a quick shot at the basket as she descended the tree.

"Thanks." He bounced the ball absently and

surveyed her. "So you're our new neighbor. We were wondering who'd bought the old Cutler place."

"Steffie Martin," she said, tilting her chin to look up at him.

"Paul Corelli." His voice was deep and she noticed long lashes shading those wonderful brown eyes that now looked dark and velvety. She especially like his eyes. Maybe it's because they're brown, she thought. She'd always liked brown eyes. She didn't know why. It was just that brown eyes made her feel soft inside, and trusting. That wasn't logical. But nevertheless, that was how brown eyes made her feel.

"You . . . uh . . . want to shoot a few baskets with me?" Paul asked.

Making up her mind instantly, Steffie took the offered basketball and announced, "We'll play HORSE." It was a universal game for basketball buffs. Shots were taken from various angles without missing the hoop until the word HORSE had been spelled by one player, making him or her the winner.

Paul's eyebrows lifted. "You first."

Steffie took her mark below the basket and made the shot with practiced ease.

Paul eyed her again. "Pretty good," he conceded.

8

. . . for a girl! Steffie finished for him in her mind. She could tell by his expression what he was thinking. "I like the game," she confessed. "I played guard on my old junior high school team."

Paul shot and the ball slipped easily through the rim of the hoop. "Since you're living here you'll be going to Madison Junior High. We have a great team. I play forward on the boys' team—the Warriors. We were All-City Champs last year. The girls' team is strong, too. Maybe you could go out for it."

Steffie took aim. She watched the ball sail through the air and settle neatly through the basket. His news interested her. She'd love to be on a good basketball team. That was one of the things she'd hated most about leaving her old school. "I may do that," she said.

Paul flashed her a grin that caused her to momentarily lose her concentration and the ball bounced off the rim instead of descending through it. Paul retrieved the ball. "I'll introduce you around to some of the gang. That way you'll know some people before school starts."

"Thanks." Steffie wanted to feel less self-conscious about the new school and new kids. Paul's offer made her feel grateful.

"You want a drink? Ma has some lemonade

in the frig. I'm thirsty and this cast weighs a ton."

Steffie followed him around to his back porch. Inside, the kitchen looked a lot like the one in her house. Except, Paul's was neat and tidy and filled with the aroma of simmering spaghetti sauce. A heavy-set woman with curly brown hair stirred a pot on the stove. She turned and faced them.

"Ma," Paul announced, crossing to the refrigerator. "This is Steffie Martin. She moved in next door."

The woman smiled and her brown eyes crinkled at the corners. "So good to meet you! Such a pretty girl! Welcome," she chattered.

Steffie blushed under her effusive words. No one ever called her pretty. "Nice to meet you, too," she mumbled.

Paul motioned toward the table. Steffie sat down as Paul placed a glass of lemonade in front of her. Steffie sipped the cold liquid and scanned the homey surroundings. The kitchen looked like a command center for a military outpost. A bulletin board spread along one wall next to the phone. A calendar, speckled with memos and notes, was pinned to the board. A chalkboard, filled with hand-written schedules, was hanging next to the board.

"When's dinner?" Paul asked.

His mother rolled her eyes. "We eat in shifts tonight. Mike has baseball practice. Denise has a date with Hal and won't be home for dinner. Tammy and Wendy are at the skating rink. Your dad's working late."

Steffie's eyes widened. Paul had such a large family! She'd often wondered what it would be like to have brothers and sisters instead of being an only child. "You have three sisters?"

Paul rolled his eyes. "Four. Francine's married. One down and three to go."

"Paul Corelli! Such a way to talk," his mother clucked cheerfully.

"Are you kidding? I have to pay a toll to use the bathroom once a day! Stockings hung all over the place, hot rollers, curling irons, hair spray . . . Why there're six kinds of shampoos in there! Mike and I are outnumbered!"

Steffie giggled, suddenly feeling very comfortable in the aromatic kitchen. The Corellis seemed like good neighbors. In a few minutes time she felt like a member of the Corelli family instead of a stranger.

"Would you like to stay for supper?" Mrs. Corelli asked.

Steffie shook her head. "Thank you, but I can't. I still have a lot to unpack and Dad's bringing dinner home."

"I'll bake a cake next week to welcome you and your family," Mrs. Corelli promised. The phone rang and she answered it. The afternoon sun flooded the kitchen with a warm light. Paul propped up his leg on another chair. Steffie smiled at him across the worn formica-topped table.

"That's Ma," Paul shrugged. "If she can't feed you, she's sure you're going to die of malnutrition." He took a long gulp from his glass and then stood. "Want to finish that game?"

"I'll beat you," Steffie said confidently.

"Fat chance!" He hobbled to the door and Steffie followed. Already she felt less lonely and more at ease in this new city, her new home. Maybe this move would be the last one for her parents. After all, they had bought a house, hadn't they? And they'd never done that before!

All at once, Steffie wanted to stay in this place. She wanted to go to the same school more than one year in a row. She wanted to have the same friends for years instead of months. She wanted to be part of a family in a regular neighborhood, full of regular people. She told herself, "Maybe this time we can stay put!"

Two

"SO what did you do this afternoon?" Steffie looked up from her paper plate, glancing at her father as she bit a chunk off the chicken leg that she was holding. Dan Martin's hair was streaked with premature gray, making him appear distinguished. To Steffie, her father's blue eyes always seemed clear and direct. It was as if he could look right through her and see into her innermost thoughts. "I met the next-door neighbors," Steffie told him. "Their name is Corelli. Paul's 14 and we'll go to the same junior high school. He's nice. I'm going out for the girls' basketball team when they have tryouts."

Dan Martin exchanged glances with his wife. "Do you think you should be making plans so far ahead?" he asked.

Stung, Steffie dropped her chicken leg and asked, "Why not? I thought we were staying here this time. I didn't think you'd buy a house just to sell it and move again."

"Now, now . . . ," her mom said soothingly. "Your father didn't mean it that way. Of course, we're staying here. I think our moving days are over."

Steffie stared at her father. His expression didn't seem half as reassuring as her mother's words. "Well?" Steffie asked. "Are we staying?"

Her father reached out and stroked her arm. "I've never done anything that wasn't in your best interests, Steffie. Always, you've come first," he said. She heard an urgency in his voice that confused her.

His answer didn't make any sense to her. How could it be good for her to move all over the country at the drop of a hat? "I like it here," she offered. "I like living in a house where I can paint my walls purple and glue posters on the walls instead of taping them or thumbtacking them. I like not having a landlord or an apartment manager telling us what we can and can't do. I like living in a real neighborhood instead of a big brick building."

Her dad laughed and the sound relieved her. She hadn't meant to sound ungrateful for the way he'd always taken care of her. "Okay, honey, I get the point," he said. "I'll take you to the paint store Saturday. You can pick out any color you want for your walls."

Steffie suppressed a relieved sigh and picked up the chicken leg again. She felt reassured and contented. Later, she spent three hard hours putting her room in order. By bedtime she had organized her desk, dresser drawers, closets, and shelves and had made up her bed with clean-smelling sheets. She fell into bed, exhausted, but pleased with herself. *Tomorrow, I'll go back over to Paul's house . . . maybe meet some of his friends,* she thought to herself.

Much later Steffie awoke vaguely disturbed, but not knowing why. The dark closed around her and shadows, cast by moonlight streaming in her window, left her disoriented. *Where am I?* She sat up in bed, remembering. It was her new house, her new city.

Voices, rising and falling, seemed to be coming from down the hallway. The muffled noise caused her to pad quietly to the door and strain to hear. Her parents were talking, arguing. She only caught snatches.

" . . . shouldn't have told her that. You can't know we won't move again."

"I'm tired, too, Dan . . . sick of moving . . . running . . . ."

"I'm doing what I have to do. You always

15

knew it might be like this. . . ."

The voices fell to a low buzz, and Steffie struggled to hear through the wooden surface of her closed door. A chill snaked through her. What were they talking about? she wondered. She was scared and unsure. She knew it wasn't right to eavesdrop. Shaking, she returned to her bed. Wiping perspiration off her forehead, she slipped between the cool sheets. It took a long time, but she finally went back to sleep.

On Saturday, her dad took her to a hardware store and she picked out paint for her bedroom walls. She decided against purple and settled on a lavender-rose that reminded her of the inside of a sea shell.

On the way home, she asked, "Did we ever live near the beach when I was little?"

"Why do you ask?" Her dad cut his eyes to her and she shrugged.

"I don't know. Sometimes I dream about playing in the ocean, but I can't ever remember going there. Sometimes I even think I smell the salt air in my sleep."

"You have a great imagination, Steffie. Sorry, but we've never lived near the sea. Not even when you were a tiny baby. Car salesmen do best in the East and Midwest, you know. That's why I've always stuck to good-sized cities. There's no time to loll around on the beach, chasing waves and blond lifeguards." He grinned sideways at her.

"When I grow up, I'm going to the beach for a vacation," she said in a matter-of-fact tone. "I think it would be fun to learn to surf, and to meet a few of those lifeguards."

"Don't get sunburned," her dad teased. "You'll turn into a lobster. And then, what will those lifeguards do?"

She reached over and pinched him playfully.

"Ouch! Watch it or I'll paint you into a corner in your room," he said.

They laughed and Steffie decided that her dad was the neatest dad in the entire world. He'd always been her friend. It was easy to talk with him and be with him. Maybe she didn't have oodles of brothers and sisters like Paul did, but she had terrific parents who loved her very much. It was enough.

* * * * *

"Hey! Anybody home?"

Steffie jerked up from her position on the sofa at the sound of Paul's voice coming from her front porch. She tossed down her book and went to the door.

Paul grinned at her through the screen.

17

"Notice anything different?"

"You've gotten a haircut."

"Very funny. My cast is off!" He beamed and she eyed his left leg, now free of its plastered burden.

"All right! Now you have no excuse when I tromp you in HORSE." She stepped out onto the porch and smiled broadly up into his big brown eyes. He smiled back and her insides went mushy again.

"Come on!" he urged. "I need to exercise my leg and build up the muscles. Let's go for a walk. There's a city park three blocks over."

Steffie told her mother she was leaving, then bounded down the porch steps and fell into stride beside Paul. They walked in the bright summer sunshine, down old cracked sidewalks, and beneath a canopy of trees that lined the walkways. The sun dappled leaf patterns over Paul's head and shoulders. Steffie felt strangely content. "Did you grow up here?" she asked.

"Never lived anyplace else," he said. Steffie almost envied him. "Where have you lived?" he asked.

"I've lost track. All I know is that we've moved a lot."

"Lucky. Wish I could say that."

She stared at him, wide-eyed. "You're

kidding! I think it's a drag to always be moving, never keeping friends longer than a few months."

"I think it would be super." He chuckled. "Ma's right. She always says, 'The grass is always greener . . . ' Still, I've never been anywhere very exciting. All Ma and Pop's families are from this area. I've never been out of Indiana."

They entered the public park. Steffie followed Paul along a winding path, noticing sloping green birms, clusters of flowering bushes, and rows of trees. A playground area hosted a pack of toddlers on swings, monkey bars, and slides. An ice cream vendor did a brisk business under the shade of a leafy oak tree. She inhaled deeply, filling her lungs with the warm air and her eyes with the variations of green colorings.

"I like it here," she said absently, not sure if she meant the park or the city.

"You want to see someplace neat?" His eyes twinkled and Steffie nodded, intrigued by his air of mystery.

She followed him off the path, through a thicket of trees, and up a craggy slope. "I found this place when I was eight. My buddies and I used to play here a lot."

He stood in front of a rock overhang and

looked around, making sure they were alone. Then he shoved aside some bushes and crouched down, wedging his shoulders into their thickness. "Come on," he urged.

Steffie knelt and crawled in after him. The bushes backed onto an indentation in the rock formation. In the dim light she could see the hollowed out scoop in the rocks. "Why, it's a cave!" she cried.

"Neat, huh?"

Steffie raised up, finding she could stand erect and walk around. She had to stoop as she neared the back of the cave. "It's great," she said. The surface of the walls was cool to her touch. But as she neared the back, it grew darker. Suddenly she felt uneasy, as if the darkness might swallow her.

"Hide, honey. Quick!"

"But it's dark and I'm scared . . ."

"Mind Mommy, honey. It's a special game between you and me. Hide and don't come out till I tell you. Promise me! Don't come out until I say it's all right."

"Hey, Steffie. Are you okay?"

She jerked around at the sound of Paul's voice. "You just kind of went blank on me, Steffie. You're not scared, are you?"

She backed toward the entrance. "Of course not." But her voice sounded quavery even to her own ears. What had she remembered . . . a conversation about hiding? Why had her mother told her to hide? she wondered.

"You look spooked," Paul said. He took her arm and pushed her through the bushes until she was once again outside in the bright warmth of the sun.

She suddenly felt stupid. "I-I don't know what happened. Something about the cave reminded me of a hiding game I once played. I'm sorry. I don't know what's going on."

Paul shrugged. "It's no big deal. Look, Steffie," he took her arm and led her back to the foot trail. "Let's just walk. There's a pond in the middle of the park I want to show you. When we get home, I'll play you a game of HORSE. Ma's baked a pie. We'll have a piece."

She agreed, grateful for his company, shaking her head to be rid of the haunting feelings of a past game she couldn't quite remember from a voice she couldn't really place.

Three

"WHERE are you going, Steffie?"

Steffie turned from her vanity mirror, setting down her can of hairspray and fanning the air with her hand to dispel the fine mist. "Why, to Paul's party, of course," she told her mother in an exasperated tone. "I told you all week that he was having some of his friends over for a party."

Her mom fidgeted. "You've been spending an awful lot of time over there, honey. You don't want to make a nuisance of yourself."

"Really, Mother! It's a party. I'm going to meet a lot of the kids I'll see at school. School starts next Monday. Besides, it's only next door." Steffie was suddenly irritated with her mother's attitude. Her mom had always been protective of her, making her stay indoors a lot as a child.

"I know. But your dad's working late and I

thought we might do something together. Maybe go to a movie."

Steffie rolled her eyes. "Mom, please. I'm only going next door for a party. It's important to me."

Alice tapped her foot, a gesture Steffie knew meant indecisiveness and confusion. "Really, Mom. I'll be fine. And I won't stay too late. We can go to a movie some other time."

Her mother gave in with a sigh. "Oh, all right. But don't go off with anyone."

Steffie picked up her purse and bounded out of her bedroom and down the stairs. She stewed inwardly during the walk to Paul's in the gathering twilight. What is with my mother anyway? she wondered. She is always warning me to "beware," to "be careful," to "never talk to strangers." Why does she treat me like a baby? "I have common sense!" she announced to the tree in Paul's yard. "Don't they trust me?"

She trotted up the Corelli back steps and knocked. Ten-year-old Tammy opened the door and pulled her into the hustle-bustle of the Corelli kitchen.

"Steffie! How pretty you look!" Mrs. Corelli beamed from her position next to the stove. "That shade of blue in your shirt certainly brings out the blue flecks in your gray eyes."

"Thank you. What's cooking?"

"Just some cookies and a few snacks."

Paul burst into the room, arms flailing. "Good grief, Ma! Tell Denise to get out of the bathroom. She's been holed up in there for an hour!"

"She has a date," Tammy announced, scooping a cookie from a serving plate.

"Those cookies are for Paul's friends. You can take cookies from this plate." Mrs. Corelli pointed to a blue-edged platter. "Denise is getting ready. Use the bathroom in the Master bedroom."

"Boy, could I tell Hal some things if he's serious about my sister," Paul grumbled. "Oh, hi, Steffie."

She flashed him a big grin, fascinated by the circuslike atmosphere of Paul's home. She still wondered what it would be like to have so much family around. I guess I'll never know, she thought. After 14 years, she doubted her parents would have any more kids.

Paul motioned her into the living room where everything looked ready and waiting for something to happen. The lamps were lit, spilling warm haloes of lights onto tabletops. A sofa and some chairs were arranged in clusters. Large floor pillows beckoned invitingly while a stereo played the newest rock tape.

"Looks great," she told him.

He nodded in agreement. "As soon as everybody arrives, I'll introduce you around. Mickey Landers plays center on the girls' basketball team. You'll like her. She'll be able to give you the scoop on the team."

Steffie grabbed a handful of roasted peanuts from a snack dish. She munched on them contentedly, listening to the sounds of bedlam in the Corelli household and feeling perfectly at home.

Paul was right about Mickey Landers. Steffie liked her a lot. Mickey was a tall girl with straight brown hair and green eyes. She was big boned and rangy, with a ready smile and a quick wit.

"The team needs a good shooter," Mickey told her. "We graduated four starters last June, so Mrs. Matasik—she's our coach—will be beating the bushes for replacements. Paul says you're pretty good from the foul line."

Steffie blushed, not from the praise—her ability to hit the mark on penalty shots was valid—but from the information that Paul considered her good enough to talk about. "I can hold my own."

"The big deal is beating the Westside Raiders. We lost to them by three baskets in the All-City Championships last spring. The whole team wants revenge!" Mickey offered a wicked smile and rubbed her hands in eager anticipation.

"I'll see if I can help avenge the Warrior name in some small way."

"Take no prisoners!" Mickey cried. Steffie felt the welling tide of school pride swell inside her. She belonged here, in this city, in this neighborhood, with these kids. She belonged! It was a wonderful feeling. She never wanted to move again.

* * * * *

Madison Junior High was an old red brick building within walking distance of Steffie's house. She liked that. She'd never been close enough to her school to walk. Either her parents had driven her, or she'd ridden a bus. This time, she went outside her door, met Paul and three of his friends, and they all walked to school together.

"You come straight home!" her mom called out through the screen door. Steffie flipped her head in defiance, hoping Paul hadn't heard her mom's anxious tone. He hadn't. They walked in good-natured conversation. Steffie listened to tales of various teachers, momentarily wishing she was a returning student instead of a new one.

But her day passed quickly and by fifth period science, she felt as if she'd gone to Madison forever. She recognized kids from Paul's party. She felt she knew teachers and office personnel by the memory of Paul's stories. In science, she encountered Paul in the same class. Mr. Wheeler, the teacher, was a short man with a thick torso and compacted energy that flowed out of his pores. He didn't talk, he exploded. "Enthusiastic," Paul whispered drily. It was an understatement.

"First, we'll study genetics," Mr. Wheeler announced. "It helps us all get an idea about where we're from . . . what we're made of."

"Protoplasm!" Herb Gallagher yelled from his desk.

The room erupted in laughter.

"Ah! But whose protoplasm?" Mr. Wheeler asked, drawing a quick diagram on the blackboard. "Here we have two parents with brown eyes. What color will their child's eye be?"

"Brown."

"According to Mendel's Law of Genetics, brown is the dominate gene. So you're right." Mr. Wheeler scribbled hastily across the board. "Two blues?" he asked.

"A blue-eyed baby."

"Blue and brown?"

The class fell silent, mulling over the options with a buzz of murmurs. Finally, Terri Franklin offered, "Either."

Mr. Wheeler grinned. "Brown still dominates. So it may be brown. Or . . . ," he paused for maximum effect, "they may be gray, a blend of brown and blue."

Blue plus blue equals blue. Blue-eyed Mom plus blue-eyed Dad equals gray-eyed Steffie. Steffie started. Something was wrong with her addition. Timidly, she raised her hand. "Can't two blues ever make another color?"

"Of course." Mr. Wheeler scratched a list of colors onto the board. "That's what makes the study of genetics so much fun. There're so many combinations. However, probability is another thing altogether. The probability is for blue-eyed babies to come from blue-eyed parents. But grandparents contribute genes, too. Hair and eye coloring can skip a generation, then bingo! Up pops a redhead from two brunettes. Just think of the possibilities! That's what we're going to study. And each of you will make a family tree. You'll learn about yourselves. Plus," he added for emphasis, "one-third of your grade in science will be based on the entire project. Think of the excitement! We'll find your roots and discover who you really are."

"Uncover skeletons!" Herb shouted to more laughter.

"In your case, Gallagher, maybe a few Frankensteins!"

Steffie squirmed, oddly ill-at-ease. Roots, she thought. Hadn't that been what she'd wanted all her young life? But this was a different kind of roots. It was heredity and lineage and family descendants. She knew that her father's parents were dead. And her mom had said her parents weren't living either. *How am I going to find my roots?* she wondered.

She looked enviously at Paul. It was so simple for him. He had plenty of family to write about on a tree chart. Maybe I'll borrow some of his, she thought absently. If she had been born a Corelli, at least she'd have brown eyes. Everyone in his family had those dark, molasses-colored eyes. For the first time in years, Steffie thought about her grandparents. Since both sets were dead, she'd never known them. I wonder what they were like? she thought. She decided to ask her dad and mom, determined that there weren't going to be any blanks on her family tree! Where had she come from anyway?

Four

"ATLANTA," Dan Martin told his daughter across the supper table. "You were born in Atlanta. And shortly thereafter, we moved to Birmingham because I was offered a better job with a big auto dealer. Why do you ask?"

Steffie felt an edge of disappointment. She knew she'd been born in Atlanta. She wanted more information, interesting things about her grandparents, aunts, uncles, and cousins. Didn't she have any? "It's for a science project," Steffie explained. "Mr. Wheeler is making all of us do family trees. And it started me thinking about my roots, about all the family I might have somewhere."

Her parents exchanged *The Look*. It was that special glance that passed between them whenever they didn't want to answer or didn't know how to answer a question she'd asked.

They used to exchange The Look a lot when she was smaller.

Steffie recognized The Look and bristled. What had brought it on? What didn't they want to tell her about their families?

"Steffie, dear," her mom began. "You know that both sets of your grandparents are deceased."

"Well, what am I going to put on my tree chart?" She sounded miffed even to her own ears.

Her father beamed her a smile. The yellow overhead light fixture sent sparkles glancing off his salt-and-pepper-colored hair. "I know plenty about my parents, and about your great-grandpa, too. He was in the Merchant Marines. He traveled around the world and spent three years in India while the British still ruled."

"You mean he saw the Taj Mahal?"

"Saw it! To hear my dad tell it, you'd have thought he built it!"

Steffie giggled, imagining a man who looked like Popeye, walking around the jungles of India while tigers slinked past him. "What about you, Mom?" She turned to her mom who dropped her eyes and set her fork down carefully.

"My forefathers weren't quite so adventuresome. My father was a mailman and Mom stayed at home. My great-grandparents immigrated from Ireland during the potato famine. They got jobs, worked hard, raised a family—pretty dull stuff. As you know, I was an only child, like you."

Steffie swallowed her disappointment. She'd hoped there might be some relatives somewhere. It would be nice to have a cousin or two.

"I had a brother," her dad ventured. Quickly Steffie turned her attention on him. "But he was killed in Viet Nam."

Steffie gasped, surprised that there had been an uncle she'd never known about. "I didn't know that."

"His name was Charles. He died two years before you were born. It's ancient history. He never married. I honestly didn't think you'd be interested in knowing."

"Is that it?"

"Is what it?"

"Is that all there is to our Family Tree?" Steffie asked.

"That's it. Sorry it's such boring stuff," her dad added.

"Well, aren't there any photos or anything?"

Steffie remembered a big box that they kept packed away in their bedroom closet. "It's full of pictures," her mom had told her once as she'd packed for a move. "Someday, I'm going to sit down and sort them out and put them into photo albums."

"I can shuffle through some old photos and see if I can find one of Charles," her dad said.

"And I'm sure I have some of my parents and our old house in Boston," her mom added.

With a start, Steffie realized she had never known her mother came from Boston. "Boston! How'd you meet Dad in Atlanta?"

Her parents exchanged The Look once more. "Alice was working as a secretary in Atlanta. She came into the car lot where I was working at the time and I sold her a car. She was so cute that I asked her for a date."

Her mom nodded with a smile. "I thought he was handsome and agreed before the words had cleared his mouth. We dated for a year, then we married."

Steffie wrinkled her nose and tapped her fingers on the tabletop, remembering their anniversary date and calculating from her birthday. She teased, "Boy, you sure didn't waste any time having me, did you?"

They glanced quickly at one another, growing suddenly tense. "Not a moment," her dad said tightly.

Something in his tone told Steffie that the

discussion was over. *Now what did I say?* she thought peevishly. One moment they'd been talking freely. The next minute, the conversation was closed. It made her angry because she had many things left to ask. Her probe into the past was over. And there was nothing she could do about it, not one single thing!

*   *   *   *   *

Steffie walked into the gym, her heart pounding, her palms perspiring. A group of girls stood around in shorts while Mrs. Matasik wrote names on her clipboard. Gerry Matasik was the tallest woman Steffie had ever seen. She towered above the eighth and ninth graders who waited to try out for the Madison girls' basketball squad.

Mickey Landers waved enthusiastically. Steffie parked her books on the wooden bleachers and walked over to Mickey's side. Her court shoes squeaked against the shiny, smooth, oak surface of the gym floor.

"I've been looking for you," Mickey said.

"I got hung up in the hall. Paul wants me to meet him and walk home after tryouts," Steffie said.

Mickey arched her brow. "Lucky you. Paul's

something else. All you did was move next door. If I'd thought of it, I'd have persuaded my folks to move the three blocks last summer when that house went up for sale."

Steffie giggled. She did feel lucky to be Paul's neighbor—and friend.

"Landers," Coach Matasik sighed. "You want to cut the jabber and take some shots from the foul line?"

"What's the matter, Coach? You afraid I lost my touch?" Mickey teased.

The coach ignored her. "Who's your friend?"

"Steffanie Martin," Steffie said.

"Position?" Coach Matasik wrote her name onto her clipboard.

"Guard."

The tall woman's eyes narrowed. "You a shooter?"

Steffie gave out her statistics. Mrs. Matasik nodded. "Impressive." She tossed Steffie a ball. "See if you can take this from half court and make it in. Landers, see if you can stop her."

The girls grinned at each other. Steffie dribbled the ball with practiced comfort and started down the court. Mickey stuck close. Steffie moved expertly toward the backboard, protecting the ball with her back and shoulders from Mickey's lunges. At the circle below the backboard, she pivoted, faked to the left, leaped, and flipped the ball effortlessly through the rim of the basket.

Mickey grinned sheepishly. "Fooled me."

"That was terrific!" Coach Matasik called. "Steffie, come back tomorrow. We'll have a practice game. I want to see you perform on the court under pressure."

Mickey flashed Steffie a grin and a thumb's up sign. Steffie smiled broadly. She'd made the first cut. And she wasn't even sweating.

* * * * *

"Hey, congratulations! I heard you made the team." Paul came up to Steffie in the hall a week later while she fiddled with the combination lock on her locker.

"Yeah, I'm pretty excited about it." Steffie smiled up at him. The list had been posted that morning. Her name, along with Mickey's and thirteen others, topped the roster for the Madison girls' squad. "Coach says we'll start practicing right after Thanksgiving."

"Your season starts in January. Ours does, too. But our practice days are different," Paul said.

"I know." She'd miss walking home with

Paul every day after school. "Coach sure sounds like she intends to win All-City Championship this year."

Paul grinned. "She's very competitive. I'll bet you all can do it, too."

"I intend to do my share."

"You ready to head home?"

She was. They fell into step together, pulling up their coat collars to the raw November wind that whipped past them in the schoolyard.

"We have a swarm of company coming for Thanksgiving," Paul told her. "Aunts, uncles, four cousins, and a dog."

"Good grief! Where will they sleep?"

"Ma always puts sleeping bags all over the living room floor. Mike and I have to give up our room for my uncle and aunt. What a drag." Leaves swirled beneath their feet. "How about you? You stuck with a bunch of family for the holidays?"

Steffie avoided his eyes, concentrating on kicking a clump of brown leaves. "Naw. Not this year."

"Lucky you," he grumbled.

"Yeah," Steffie echoed. "Lucky me."

They stepped off a curb and turned toward their street. A shaft of late afternoon sunlight glanced off a car windshield, causing Steffie to blink. A plain white sedan, parked on the opposite side of the street, caught her attention. The car looked non-descript and colorless. A man in a black overcoat leaned back against the seat, as if he were asleep. She thought it strange he'd sit in a cold car on such a cold day.

"Want to shoot some baskets when we get home?" Steffie asked.

"Sure. Come over for hot chocolate first. We need to toast your making the team." Paul winked.

Steffie gave a self-conscious shrug, passing by the car and the man without a backward glance.

Five

OVER the Thanksgiving holidays Paul's house filled to overflowing with relatives. Steffie watched from her bedroom window as doors slammed and kids ran helter-skelter on the Corellis' lawn. She shot baskets with Paul in the late afternoons while wide-eyed children watched. Her aim was off because of the clothes that bundled around her. But the kids didn't notice.

"You have a nice bunch of relatives," she told him.

"Another bunch will be here for Christmas. How do you spell relief?"

"How?" Steffie asked.

"N-o-k-i-d-s."

She chuckled. "But they adore you. Hero worship and all that stuff."

He leaned over with a conspiring look. "I'll sell you a few. Think of what great tree ornaments they would make."

After Thanksgiving the days seemed to hurdle, non-stop toward Christmas. At school Steffie began practicing with the team, anticipating the start of the season in late January. When Christmas break arrived, she went with her dad to pick out a tree. The three of them spent one evening decorating it.

Remembering the clamor around the decorating party at the Corelli house, her own family's efforts seemed forced and quiet. Her mom popped popcorn and Steffie strung it on a string, alternating the fluffy white kernels with red cranberries. She wanted it to be fun, but she realized that there wasn't much in the way of family traditions to excite her.

The Christmas before they'd lived in Connecticut. The one before that, Chicago. It was hard to keep track. The contrast between her and the Corellis households was dramatic. At the Corellis there was always something going on, always something happening. The Corellis' house was always filled with the aromas of rich foods and baking cookies. Denise made a gingerbread house. Paul nibbled off a corner of the roof. She chased him around the large house with a pancake turner.

The tree soared to the ceiling in the Corelli

living room, heavy with handmade ornaments and sparkling glass balls. Streamers flanked the fireplace mantle ladened with Christmas cards. More relatives arrived, including a brown-eyed little four-year-old named Angela who hung on Steffie, following her around like a puppy. She could be my sister, Steffie thought.

"How come we don't have Christmas cards hanging over our fireplace?" she asked her dad one night. All the cards they'd received for the holidays sat in a small clump on the coffee table. Absently, she leafed through them. One was from her dad's boss. One was from the Corellis. Another was from their bank and their paperboy. She plopped them onto the table. Dull.

Her dad gazed over the edge of this newspaper. "Never kept track of people that much. We've moved a lot. Never bothered to send cards either."

Steffie crossed her arms and stared into the fireplace . . . gas logs. Even the fire wasn't real. "Rotten reasons," she mumbled.

"Aren't we testy," her dad chided. "Christmas is coming. You want me to give Santa a bad report?"

"Oh, Daddy!" she tried to keep the corners of her mouth from turning up.

"Come here, honey."

She sidled toward him. He draped his arm over her shoulders. "You have the Christmas blahs. A lot of people get them. Too much holiday."

She wanted to tell him it was more than that. She wanted to tell him that she felt sort of lonely, but she didn't know how. Besides, her feelings didn't make sense. "I like it here," she blurted.

"It's a nice place," her dad agreed.

"Do you like your job?" questioned Steffie.

"Yes."

"A lot?"

"Are you worried that we're going to move away again?" he asked.

Her dad had seen into the core of her feelings. "It's crossed my mind," Steffie said.

"I'm content. It looks as if we'll stay put. If it will make you feel better, your mom's going to take a job as a secretary. After the first of the year, she's going to work in the offices across the street from the car lot I manage."

Steffie blinked with surprise. "She is?"

"Hey—you're fourteen."

"Almost fifteen," she corrected.

"Alice wants to work. How do you feel about it?"

Steffie was delighted. The more roots they

put down, the better the chances they'd stay, she thought. "I think it's a good idea. I have practice after school two days a week. Most days I don't even get home til five o'clock."

"And we'll be home by six. It's a convenient job for her. We can leave together and come home together. You'll be waiting for us for a change. How does that sound?"

Steffie grinned fully while staring into his blue eyes. "I think it's super. Maybe I can start supper for us sometimes."

He squeezed her shoulders. "You're worth all the sacrifices, Steffie."

She knitted her brow and gave him a puzzled look. "What sacrifices?"

He chucked her chin fondly. "Someday I'll tell you. But right now let's just enjoy the fire."

She gazed back at the blazing logs, more than a little confused by her dad's comment. But she didn't dwell on it. Her mom was going to work. Maybe they were finally putting down permanent roots. Maybe they'd be here for the next Christmas, too.

* * * * *

Paul spun the basketball around on the tip of his index finger, balancing it while letting it whirl. Steffie watched Angela watch the spinning ball. "She's such a cute little girl," she told herself.

Icicles hung off the orange rim of the basketball hoop. It was too cold and too slick to shoot, so Steffie and Paul stood making steam with their breaths.

"Hey, Angie," Paul said. "Are all those tears dried up yet?"

Solemnly, the child nodded, wiping her nose on the back of her mitten. She sniffed and thrust out her lower lip. "They won't let me play with them."

"Who won't?" Paul asked.

Angela listed the names of her and Paul's sisters.

"What are they playing?" Steffie asked.

"Hide and seek."

"Why won't they let you play?" Paul asked, concerned.

"Because I can't find good places to hide. I hid under the kitchen table, but Wendy saw me right away and started laughing! She called me a dummy, too!"

"But, Angie," Paul said gently, "there's no cloth covering the kitchen table. Of course, they could see you."

"See what I mean!" Angela wailed. "I can't find any good places!"

"Listen, why don't I help you find a place?" Steffie made the offer and watched Angela's brown eyes light up.

"Will you?"

"Of course. Come on. Let's go tell the other girls." Steffie took the child's mittened hand and led her inside Paul's house. The scent of cinnamon and nutmeg filled the air of the room. They tracked down Angela and Paul's sisters and told them their plan. The older girls agreed, awed by Steffie's offer to become a part of their play.

Once Wendy started counting, Steffie pulled Angela down the hallway, searching for a good hiding place. She spied it in the hall closet. Not only was the closet roomy, but there was a big empty box marked "Christmas Decorations." Steffie tucked Angela inside the box. "Now don't make a sound," Steffie cautioned.

"Don't leave me!" Angela grasped her hand and clung tightly. "It's dark in here."

Flustered, Steffie hadn't considered that she'd have to hide with the child. She started to refuse, but quickly saw new tears brim in Angela's eyes. "Oh, all right!" she agreed. "Scoot over." Steffie climbed into the huge cardboard box, too. Together, the girls controlled their giggles as they heard the others running past the door looking for them.

Once, Wendy even opened the closet door, but she didn't look into the box, so she missed them.

Steffie felt the confinement in cramped leg muscles. She wanted to stand and stretch, but she didn't want to give away their location.

"Hide, honey! Quick! Under the bed."

"But it's dark under there."

"I know. But it's very important that you mind Mommy and don't come out til I tell you."

Steffie shook her head to rid herself of the snatches of some long ago conversation she couldn't understand. Why did her mom want her to hide? "I think we fooled them, Angela," Steffie said suddenly in the dark space.

"Oh, not yet, Steffie. Let's not go out yet. Let's make them look some more."

"No!" Steffie snapped, then regretted it. She gentled her tone. "No, I have to go home now. The game's over. And you won."

She helped the child out of the box. She took deep shuddering breaths to calm her nerves before they emerged from the closet to claim their victory.

*   *   *   *   *

Steffie wandered around her house, listlessly dusting the furniture. She was glad that the holidays were almost over. Personally, she was bored. She wanted to return to school and classes and basketball practice. "I'm a traitor to all kids," she admitted aloud, " but I can't wait for Monday morning."

"Are you using the spray wax?" her mom's voice called down from the upstairs level.

Hastily, Steffie scooped up the can and sprayed a fine film of lemon scented mist onto the coffee table. "Yes, Mom!" She looked out the window. Unusually bright rays from a January sun left the snow on the front lawn dazzling. If the sun shone all day, the newly fallen snow would be melted by afternoon. If so, maybe she and Paul could shoot some baskets. With all his relatives gone, time hung heavy on his hands, too.

Steffie approached her parents' desk and looked at the surface with dismay. It was piled with papers, bills, and file folders marked "Income Tax." "How am I supposed to dust around this mess?" she griped.

"Don't forget to do upstairs, too!" her mom's voice drifted down to her.

"Yes, Mom!" With a grumble, Steffie began shuffling papers, stacking them in neat little piles, exposing the desk top for her dust cloth. Her eyes fell onto a letter newly started in her mother's handwriting. It was obvious that her mom had started it, gotten distracted, and left it to do something else. Steffie would have never noticed it—never even been interested in it—except for the words that leaped off the beige linen-look stationery. In her neat and precise penmanship, her mother had penned in black ink:

January 2

Dear Mom and Dad,

We had a good holiday. I only wish we could have shared it with you. Don't worry. Things continue to go smoothly. . . .

Six

THE words stabbed at Steffie's eyes and bands tightened around her chest. It was difficult to breathe. She re-read the paper. She remembered her mom's words just a few weeks earlier: *"You know that both sets of your grandparents are deceased."* Her mother had lied to her! Lied! And her father had let her lie. Why?

With shaking hands, Steffie organized the papers, shoving the incriminating partial letter under a stack. She backed away from the desk. Her eyes stung and she felt cold inside. Her grandparents weren't dead. Yet, her parents wanted her to think that they were. It didn't make any sense.

She thought of her parents moving from city to city. She remembered the conversation she'd overheard, half-asleep, one night way back in August. What had she heard? Steffie puckered her brow, forcing up the memory. Her mother had said, " . . . sick of moving . . . running. . . ." Her father had said, "You always knew it might be this way."

Maybe they're running from the police! Steffie's eyes widened at the idea. Her parents? Criminals? It couldn't be true! She shook her head to dispel the horrible thought. No. There had to be a better explanation. But try as she might, Steffie couldn't think of one. She couldn't think of a single reason why they had told her—made her believe—that her grandparents were dead.

That night at the supper table, Steffie moved her food around on her plate, unable to look her parents in the eye. She had no appetite. She felt like her insides were ready to explode.

"Don't you like the meat loaf, honey?" her mom's voice asked.

"It's fine." The air hung tense with the weight of Steffie's short answer.

"Do you feel all right? Is something bothering you?" It was her father's turn to ask.

Everything! "Nothing."

"You seem very withdrawn tonight, Steffie," her mom said.

Steffie slammed her fork down. "Why did you tell me my grandparents were dead? If they are, why did you write a letter to dead people?" The hot words erupted out of Steffie's mouth before she could stop them. She felt herself shaking all over. But she refused to take them back.

She watched as her parents exchanged shocked glances. "Were you snooping?" her father asked. His tone was quiet, accusing.

"I wasn't snooping!" Steffie shot back. "I was dusting the desk. I saw Mom's letter. You lied to me! Both of you! Why?" Tears threatened.

"Oh, no!" her mom gasped. "I didn't think . . . I-I mean, I didn't realize. . . ."

Dan Martin shot her a look, cleared his throat and came around the table. He knelt in front of Steffie's chair and tried to take her hands into his. She pulled away.

"Sweetheart, please listen to me. There's a good explanation," he began.

"I couldn't think of a single one!"

Her dad's light blue eyes took on a look of tenderness. "Stop pulling away, Steffie. Let me explain."

She slumped, but she kept watching his face, warily. He took her hands, running his thumbs over her palms. "When your mother and I got married, her parents weren't very pleased about it. In fact, they were downright

51

angry. They were so angry that they disowned their own daughter. Do you know what that means?"

Steffie found her voice. "They didn't want to see her again?"

"That's right."

"But why?" Her voice cracked.

He shrugged. "It's just the way people get sometimes when they don't want their child to do something against their will. So we respected their wishes. We didn't bother them."

"But when I was born . . . "

"Even then." He sounded sad. "We didn't want you to think that it had anything to do with you. So we just told you they were dead."

"But it was a lie."

"Yes. Forgive us for that."

"You-you still write them?" Steffie turned toward her mother, seeing her eyes grow hard and her lips pressed into a fine line.

"Yes," she said crisply. "I keep in touch . . . in case they ever decide to change their minds and take me back." The tone of her voice sounded angry and her eyes never left her husband's face.

Steffie's dad ignored her and forced Steffie to look at him again. "Will you forgive me, Steffie? I—We never meant to hurt you."

Dumbly, Steffie nodded. Her anxiety didn't leave. She didn't like the explanation, but she didn't question it. What kind of parents could disown their own daughter? Suddenly, she felt sorry for her mother, imagining how she must feel.

Steffie's dad pulled her against his chest and smoothed her hair. "See? There's no reason to not eat supper and be glum. Everything's fine, honey. Perfectly fine," he reassured her.

But later that night, after she'd gone up to bed, Steffie lay awake in the dark for a long time. She didn't want to sleep. She wanted to think. She believed her father. But there had been a look on her mother's face that had made her feel uneasy.

Steffie heard the rise and fall of their voices from the living room below. She crept to her door, out into the hall and to the edge of the banister, not intending to eavesdrop, yet compelled to do so. The dim light from the hall lamp cast long shadows across the braided rug in the foyer.

She heard her mother's voice rise. "You had the perfect opportunity to tell her, Dan. Why didn't you? Why?"

"I'll tell her when I'm good and ready."

"For heaven's sake. She's almost fifteen

years old. It's about time she knew the truth!"

"Don't push me, Alice. I've sacrificed too much to loose it all now. She's *my* daughter. And I'll tell her in *my* time."

Steffie pressed her back against the wall, feeling the hardness through her flannel night gown. Tell me what, Daddy? she wondered. There were so many secrets, so many lies. Steffie felt like a fly caught in a spider's web. She backed into her bedroom and cried herself to sleep against her pillow.

* * * * *

"Martin! Landers! What's with you two today?" Coach Matasik barked after a blast from her whistle stopped the practice mid-court in the school gym. "For crying out loud, Steffie! You've been letting Mickey run all over you. Where's that cut and turn move you do so well?"

Steffie leaned over, resting her hands against her knees and taking in deep breaths. How could she tell Coach that her mind wasn't on the practice. And it wasn't on the upcoming game with Dunlop Junior High.

"The season opens tomorrow afternoon and you're asleep on the court. What gives?" Coach Matasik tapped her toe impatiently on the hardwood floor and stared down expectantly at Steffie.

"Sorry, Coach," Steffie mumbled. "I'll get it together by tomorrow. Promise."

Coach Matasik softened her voice and tapped Steffie on the shoulder. "Let's wrap it up for the day. Maybe I've gotten everybody too keyed up about tomorrow's game."

The team trotted into the locker room, Steffie in the lead. She jerked open her locker and removed her street clothes. She changed quickly, avoiding Mickey's questioning gaze. She couldn't forget her parents' deceptions. Now, her mom was at work every afternoon and Steffie went home to an empty house. She didn't mind. But there was too much time to think.

What had her mom meant when she'd said to her dad, "You had the perfect opportunity to tell her the truth." The truth about what? What don't I know? she wondered. It was slowly driving Steffie crazy.

Steffie crunched home in the winter's afternoon air. Slushy snow lined the sidewalks. Barren trees stood like silent soldiers along the easement.

"Hey! Steffie! Wait up!"

She turned to see Paul jogging toward her, his books tucked under his arm. His silver ski jacket made his shoulders look broad. His dark hair poked out from under his black knit hat. The cold air reddened his cheeks and his brown eyes danced in chocolate sparkles. Seeing him made her stomach do funny quivers. "Why're you leaving so late today?" Steffie asked.

He fell into step beside her. "Mr. Walters caught me passing notes in class and made me stay after. How'd practice go?"

She shrugged. "I was off. Lucky you. You've already played and won your first game."

"By this time tomorrow, you'll be able to say the same thing." He grinned down at her.

She scuffed the snow with her boot and shrugged.

"How's your Family Tree project coming?" he asked.

"Fine," she lied. In fact, she'd shoved it aside in her mind and refused to think about it.

"If I hang one more relative on mine, a branch will break."

She smiled. He continued. "Did I tell you about my Uncle Lucas? He was a sheepherder over in Italy. When he came to America he couldn't find any sheep, so he sent for some. He tried to keep them in his apartment in New York. The health department made him move.

56

Can you imagine? Sheep in the hallways of a New York apartment?" Paul laughed aloud.

Steffie wondered what it would be like to have crazy relatives, *any* relatives. "My ma let me look through some old photos," Paul said, snapping her out of her black thoughts. "I saw a picture of my great-grandmother on her wedding day. She was only four-foot-ten!" He shook his head.

Steffie snapped to attention. The old photos! Of course! Her dad had promised to look through them for her. Maybe she'd feel better if she could actually see the people from her family history. Her grandparents . . . her dead uncle . . . herself as a baby. Maybe it would settle her feelings of uneasiness, of deception.

At her walkway, Steffie told Paul good-bye and bounced up her porch steps feeling better than she had in days. She rummaged through her purse for her house key. A reflection from the street shimmered in the glass storm door and caught her eye. There was a white car and a man in a black overcoat. Something nagged in the back of her mind.

Steffie furrowed her brow. Something seemed familiar. She couldn't decide what. She turned to get a closer look, but the man slipped the car into gear and drove it quickly down the street. She watched it disappear, wondering again where she'd seen it before. She shrugged and slipped into the warmth of her home.

Seven

"THIS is all you could find?" The disappointment in Steffie's voice was apparent even to her own ears.

Her father patted her back and leaned closer to her on the sofa. He spread out the dozen photos on the coffee table in front of them. "What gratitude!" his voice teased. "Why, I dug through piles of junk to find these heirlooms for you."

Steffie scanned the handful of old photos, struggling with a sense of frustration. She'd expected more than these few photos of her relatives. She picked up one. "Is this Uncle Charles?"

A youthful face in an army uniform grinned back at her. "Yes. He was only eighteen there. He died in Viet Nam three years later."

She lay it down and picked up another. Two older people, a man and a woman, stood in front of a white framed two-story house with a steep pitched roof. "Alice's parents," her dad told her. "Emma and Lew Rielly."

Steffie stared at them for a long time. The faces looked fuzzy and out of focus. She wished the photo was clearer.

"These were my parents." Her father handed her a photo of two people in front of an old storefront.

"Where are they?"

"St. Louis. Dad owned a meat market there."

"Are they really dead?"

"Yes," he said quietly. "They're really dead."

She felt ashamed momentarily for asking the question. "Who's this?" She held another picture up to the light and saw a much younger version of her father in a basketball uniform.

"Why, that's the crack center for the St. Louis High School Panthers! Surely, you recognize that manly stance. It used to strike terror into the hearts of opponents."

"Oh, Daddy!"

"You laugh! How dare you!" His eyes twinkled. In the next moment he'd pounced on Steffie and began tickling her.

Steffie shrieked and twisted away from his

tickling fingers. Pictures went flying as they sprawled and tumbled onto the floor. After a few minutes, they lay together in a heap of giggling exhaustion. Steffie propped herself up onto her elbow and picked up a picture of herself. She was seven in the old photo, smiling a gap-toothed grin off the paper. "Boy, was I ugly!"

"Never!" her father countered. "You were beautiful!"

Steffie wrinkled her nose and tossed the picture aside. She rose to her knees and gathered the scattered snapshots. Except for the photo of Charles and the two of her grandparents, she saw nobody new. "How about more baby pictures of me?"

Her dad rose to his feet, avoiding her eyes. "We lost most of them during our many moves." He dusted off his slacks.

Her mouth dropped open. "You mean, you don't have any baby pictures of me?"

"Sorry, honey." He reached down and tossled her hair. "Can't seem to find a thing before you were seven."

"Nothing?"

"Not a thing." He raked his hand through his thick hair. "Take what you want to paste on your Family Tree chart. I-uh-promised your mother I'd do a project in the basement."

"But, Daddy! There's so much more I want to know!" Steffie wailed.

He shrugged his shoulders. "Sorry, honey. Can't talk now. Maybe later."

Slightly stunned and feeling cheated, Steffie watched him leave the room. She'd seen a few photographs and still knew nothing more than she had weeks before. It wasn't fair!

She picked up the high school photo of her father and stared at his youthful grin, struggling to see herself in his facial features. After a long time, she stacked it with the others neatly on the coffee table.

* * * * *

Steffie caught the basketball, pivoted, and raced down the court. She dribbled the ball in front of her, avoiding the forward on the opposing team, attempting to steal the ball from her. Beneath the home basket, Steffie drew up short, lunged, and slipped the ball neatly through the overhead ring. A cheer sounded from the spectators in the gym as two more points went on the board for the Madison Junior High Warriors.

"Nice work!" Gerry Matasik called from her position at the sidelines. Steffie backed toward the girl she guarded. When the ball came in from out of bounds, she managed to get her fingertips on it, stealing it out from under the opposition's noses. Another cheer erupted from the crowd as she went in for the lay-up and came down with two more points for her team.

Quickly, she eyed the scoreboard. Less than a minute in the game and the Warriors were up by nine goals. Fifty-five seconds later, the referee's whistled blasted and Steffie's team trotted off the court amid cheers, victors of their fifth straight game.

"We're hot stuff!" Mickey yelled above the shouts in the gym, a grin on her sweat-streaked face.

Steffie flashed her a thumbs-up sign and flopped onto the team bench. She wiped her face and neck with a towel. Her teammates crowded around her, praising her skilled play that had once again led them to a school victory.

"You were all terrific!" Coach Matasik shouted. "I smell the All-City trophy from here!"

"But it's only mid-season!" Dottie, the big center, said.

Mickey peered into the water bucket. "Ah, yes! But Madame Landers sees 'Championship' in our future."

"Gee, all I see is soggy towels," Steffie quipped, looking over the edge of the pail.

The team laughed. "Hey, Steffie!" Paul's familiar voice called to her, and she glanced up, seeing him standing on a descending row of bleachers. He bounded down the wooden benches, followed by two guys from the boys' team. "Nice game!" he added, landing next to her on the floor.

She felt suddenly self-conscious, remembering how she must look, stained with perspiration, her hair in damp clumps. Several elbows from her teammates poked in her ribs.

"Guess we'll hit the showers," Mickey said with a great display of leaving.

Steffie watched the team head for the locker room. She stood, hugging the towel tighter to her neck, hoping her deodorant was still effective. "Do you want to go get a drink?" Paul asked.

"Uh—sure. But I need to change. Can you wait?"

He nodded. "You really played a great game."

She swelled inside. "I'll be out in a minute." She started toward the locker room when another voice stopped her.

"Great game, honey."

"Dad!" Steffie was genuinely surprised. Her

father rarely attended the games in the late afternoon. "You got off work, just to see me play?" She beamed.

"I told them that my little girl was burning up the courts and I wasn't about to miss one more game." He shrugged and grinned. "What could they say except, 'Take the rest of the day off.'"

"That's super. Thanks."

"Can I buy you a soda?" her dad asked.

She glanced at Paul. "Uh—well—gee. . . ." her cheeks flamed.

For the first time, her dad noticed Paul. Realization dawned and he jammed his hands in his pockets with an understanding look. "I see. It seems I asked too late."

Steffie shuffled her feet. Paul said, "Hey. No problem, Mr. Martin. I'll catch you later, Steffie."

Steffie swallowed, torn between wanting him to stay and watching him leave. "Did your old dad mess up your date?" her father asked after Paul had gone.

Her face flushed hotly again. "It wasn't a date. We're just friends."

Steffie's dad looked at her for a long moment. "Sorry, honey. I guess you're not really 'my little girl' any more. So much has changed since you were a kid." A strange look crossed his face that Steffie couldn't read. What did he mean?

"Your invitation still open for that soda?" She attempted to brush aside the moment of awkwardness between them.

"Of course." His easy-going grin returned.

Together they crossed the gymnasium. The arena was empty except for a lone janitor who was preparing to buff the oak floor. "Steffie! Wait up."

Gerry Matasik's voice haulted their progress to the locker room. Now what? Steffie thought crossly. At this rate she'd never get to the showers.

Coach Matasik loped up to Steffie and her father, leading another woman behind her. "I want you to meet Darcy Hardin," the coach said.

Steffie and her dad smiled at the small redheaded woman in a crisp, fresh, emerald green business suit. "Darcy is a sports reporter for the city newspaper," Coach Matasik continued enthusiastically. "And guess what? They want to do a feature article on our girls' basketball team in next Thursday's edition. Isn't that great?"

Ms. Hardin held out her hand. Steffie took it timidly, noticing the long red, perfectly manicured nails. "How are you, Steffie? My, that was some game you played today."

"Thank you." Steffie thought, You don't look like a sports reporter.

As if reading her mind, Ms. Hardin offered, "I never played basketball. But I was quite a swimmer. I love sports and have been a reporter covering sports action for five years now."

"What do you want with Steffie?" Dan Martin asked the question. Steffie noticed that his body had grown tense and rigid, his clear blue eyes wary and clouded.

"Why, I want to do a feature article on her for my youth sports column—photos, interview—the works. She's a terrific player and deserves to be recognized. The high school coaches already have their eyes on her."

Surprised and pleased, Steffie turned excitedly toward her father. But the look on his face killed the delight within her in one instant. "It's absolutely out of the question," Dan Martin said coolly. "I don't want Steffie featured."

"But, Mr. Martin," Coach Matasik gasped.

"But, Dad," Steffie whispered.

"I said, 'No'. And I mean it!" He turned to his shocked daughter. "Now get your things and come home with me right now. You can take a shower when we get home."

She opened her mouth to protest, unable to believe what he'd told them. "I said, 'Now', Steffie. There will be no newspaper story featuring you. And that's final."

Eight

STEFFIE sat in the car in numb silence during the ride home. She kept her eyes riveted on the outside scenery, watching the snowy landscape pass, yet not really seeing it. A fine mist of tears veiled her vision. She wasn't upset about not being in the story. No. It wasn't that. It was the way her father had acted, the way he'd refused the offer. What could it matter if her picture was in the newspaper? Why didn't he want her featured?

"Are you still speaking to me?" her dad's voice startled her.

She sniffed, but ignored him.

"Come on, honey." He reached across the brown plush car seat for her hand. She pulled away from his grasp.

"Steffie," he pleaded. "Don't be angry. I have good reasons for not wanting publicity."

"I can't think of a single one!" she snapped.

"Look, baby. It's a mean world out there. There're a lot of kooks and crazies running around. I don't believe in spotlighting our family in the public eye. Is it so terrible that I want to protect you?"

Open-mouthed, she stared at him. "You're afraid someone will kidnap me?"

"Maybe."

"That's the craziest thing you've ever said to me!"

"A parent can't be too cautious," he defended.

"I'm too old to take candy from strangers, Daddy! And I know all the rules about getting into strange cars and never letting phone callers know I'm home alone. I'm not a baby!"

He attempted to pat her hand. "Of course you're not. You're my daughter. And I don't ever want anything to happen to you."

"Well, I doubt that some child stealer is going to read about me and my school basketball team in the newspaper and come take me!" she huffed, flouncing her long hair over her shoulder.

Dan Martin rotated his shoulders in a gesture of weariness. "You'd be surprised. . . ." He let the statement trail and Steffie surveyed him through narrowed eyes. His knuckles were white from gripping the steering wheel.

Suddenly, he looked tired and drained. She didn't understand one thing he was talking about. She only knew that something wasn't right. And it was something deep, dark, and scary. She didn't know what to do about it.

* * * * *

"Are you going to eat the rest of your fries?" Paul asked over the table at the restaurant.

"No." Steffie watched him take the bag and remove the remainder of her French fries. She watched him, the late afternoon sun flicking light patterns off his dark hair. If her mind hadn't been elsewhere, this afternoon would have been at the top of her list for exciting moments. She was alone with Paul, sharing hamburgers and drinks while half the student body of Madison Junior High flowed in and out of the restaurant, observing them.

"So, aren't you going to tell me what a great game I played?" Paul questioned, gulping down a swig of his drink.

"You know you played a great game." She wrinkled her nose at him.

"Nine wins in a row. Even the girls' team can't say that!"

"We've only lost one," Steffie defended. "Besides, you started your season before us."

"So what's bugging you?" His question caused her to drop her gaze and stare at the smooth formica tabletop. "I know something's bothering you, Steffie. And it isn't the basketball season."

She gave him a little half-smile. Paul could read her moods easily. Over the months, he had become her closest friend. They walked to school together, had science class together, shot baskets in his side yard over the weekends, and had many of the same friends. Suddenly, she wanted to talk to him about her mixed-up feelings about her family. "Did you ever think your parents were hiding something from you?" she asked, feeling her heart hammer and her mouth go dry.

Paul tipped his head quizzically. "Yeah, when my mom was going to have her last baby. She and Dad tip-toed around not telling me for months. But when I saw her knitting booties . . . What do you think they are hiding?"

"Not something little like that, but something big. Something . . . weird."

"Hey! I have four sisters! Another baby's a big deal!" He joked, but failed to erase the frown from her face. "You're serious, aren't you? Tell me about it."

Steffie sighed. "It's crazy, but I hear them

talking sometimes. Mom tells Dad to tell me the truth about something. And they have always told me that my grandparents were dead. But then I find out that my mom's parents are still alive. They just aren't speaking to us. And then all the moving we've done. Every year it's a new city, a new school. And the other day Dad about blew a fuse when the newspaper wanted to do that story on the girls' basketball team, featuring me. None of it makes any sense." She stopped talking, realizing that her words were tumbling into one another.

Paul pursed his lips. "Parents don't need reasons to act strange, you know. I'm sure there's a good explanation."

"Can you think of one?" Silence. "Me either."

Paul drummed his fingers against the tabletop. The noise began to irritate her. "You think they're hiding something about the past? Something they don't want you to know?" he asked.

"Yes." Her voice was barely a whisper. "Paul, what if it's something horrible? What if they're criminals?" She scanned his face for a long time. Her heart thudded. Having finally said it, Steffie realized what her greatest fear was. *What if they are hiding from the police?*

she wondered. She needed answers.

"Your dad has a full-time job, Steffie. You're enrolled in a public school. Your Mom works. It doesn't seem like they're 'hiding out' to me."

She went limp with relief. *Of course. Paul makes good sense. How could they be hiding from the police if they're so visible and involved with common, ordinary things?* "Thanks," she told him. "I—I don't know what to think about it, that's all."

He stretched his arms overhead and leaned back against his chair. "It's strange. But don't let it get to you. Besides, are you sure you really want to know? What if you discover something you can't handle?"

She stared at him. "Like what?"

"Who knows? But you have to decide whether to tell them what you're thinking and make them talk straight to you. Or you can go on wondering and living in the pits about it."

Paul was right and she knew it. She wasn't a kid anymore and things were going on about which she needed to know. One way or the other, she'd have to get her parents to talk to her.

"Are you ready to walk home?" Paul stood and slipped his arms into his ski jacket.

Steffie stood and tugged on her coat, too.

How bad can things be? she wondered. She was almost fifteen, a starter on her school's basketball team, and she was walking home with Paul Corelli. From the corner of her eye, Steffie saw two tables of seventh and eighth grade girls look her way with envy. Paul held the door for her and together they walked out of the restaurant.

* * * * *

"Hiding? What makes you think we're hiding something from you, Steffie?" Her father's voice sounded casual, but Steffie saw the signs of wariness around his eyes. She stood in the living room, facing them as her dad read the paper and her mother did some mending. Steffie noticed that her question had caused her mother's hands to stop in mid-air.

"I don't know," Steffie confessed, feeling suddenly foolish for having asked in the first place.

"Well, it's a preposterous notion," her dad said smoothly. "I admit that we've moved around a lot and we're protective of you. But we're certainly not hiding anything from you."

With a jerky motion, her mom flung down her mending and stood. Steffie started with surprise because her mom's face appeared troubled, her mouth tight and drawn. "What's wrong, Mom?"

"I just thought of something I need to do upstairs," she said crisply. Her husband shot her The Look. But she ignored him and quickly left the room.

"I didn't mean to upset her," Steffie said, stricken.

"She had a rough day at work. Don't worry about it." He held out his hand and Steffie took it. "Please put all these notions out of your head. There's nothing wrong. And we're not hiding anything from you."

Steffie allowed him to pull her down onto his lap and hug her. But nothing was different and she knew it. They had told her nothing. In fact, her mother's actions had only deepened the mystery. She'd have to think of another way of finding out.

* * * * *

Steffie stepped out into the late afternoon sunlight from the school gym and onto the deserted school yard. She inhaled the fragrant air, faint with the blush of spring, filling her lungs. She was glad to be free of the stale smell of sweat and gym shoes. The practice had run longer than usual. With the regular season over, and the All-City Championships about to begin, Coach Matasik was working the team harder than ever.

"She wants that trophy," Mickey had said minutes before in the locker room. "According to the rules, we have to play in the round-robin. We all know it's going to come down to us and Westside, just like last year. Except this year, Coach intends to win, even if it kills us!" Mickey had groaned.

The school year had flown—only two more months left. "And the All-City Championship Tournament," Steffie said aloud. And a term paper, final exams, and my dumb Family Tree! She made a face, remembering that she still hadn't done anything constructive on the project. It would count for a third of her grade for the year!

At the crosswalk, Steffie glanced both ways down the empty street. At least the days were getting longer again and night didn't come so early. With both her parents working, she had time and daylight enough to shoot baskets with Paul before setting the table for supper.

A parked automobile on the far side of the street caught her eye. Something pricked at her mind, something familiar. *Now where have I seen that car before?* She stopped short and gazed at the vehicle for a full minute. The car was new and white—a sedan. Steffie froze. A man in a dark trench coat sat behind the wheel. And he was watching her!

Nine

STEFFIE ran. She raced down the street, clutching her books to her chest, the wind stinging her face, her heart thumping and pounding. She ran until she felt as if her lungs would burst, until her legs wobbled, weak and rubbery. She ran until she hit her front porch. She tore at the storm door, wrenching it open. She fumbled in her purse for her key, all the while glancing over her shoulder for the white sedan and its driver.

Her hands shook and trembled as she inserted the key into the lock. Finally the door swung open and Steffie heaved inside, slamming the door and locking it quickly from within. The house hunkered . . . empty and silent. All she heard were her own ragged breaths and the ticking of the hall clock. Sweat trickled down between her shoulder blades. Beads of moisture collected on her face and scalp. Her fear tasted metallic in her mouth.

Who . . . who was that man? Why. . . why was he staring at me? I've seen him before. He's been watching me all along! Nausea clutched at her stomach and she felt sick and weak. She dropped her books on the floor with a thud. She turned, pressing her body against the cool, hard surface of the wall, next to the window. Cautiously, she pulled back the curtain and peeked outside. The street in front of her house was empty. There was no sign of the white sedan.

Steffie's knees shook from tension and her heart slowly regained its normal rhythm. She hurried upstairs to her bedroom window. She carefully raised the shade in front of the dainty lavender voile curtains and looked again at the street below. Lengthening shadows crawled across the pavement in the waning light.

"It was my imagination," she told her collection of basketball trophies. But she knew it hadn't been. No . . . the man in the white car definitely had been watching her. "Spying on me!" she amended aloud. But why? *Why?*

"I'll tell Dad!" The sound of her own voice comforted her and helped quell her fear. But if she did, would he make them move again? Would he think it was some kidnapper and make her pack and move? Steffie chewed on her lower lip, hesitant, scared, confused, unsure of what to do. "I don't want to move away. I don't!"

She glanced out the window one more time. This time she leaned forward until she could scan the old residential street from corner to corner in both directions. Nothing was out of the ordinary. Nothing was suspicious. The car was nowhere in sight. She couldn't prove a thing. Ultimately, she decided to say nothing. It would only upset her parents and possibly make them overreact.

"I'll tell Paul," she decided. "Tomorrow—after school—when we walk home. If the car's there, I can show him and he'll tell me what to do. Yes . . . I'll wait and tell Paul." Certain of her choice, Steffie headed back downstairs toward the kitchen and dining room to set the table for supper.

* * * * *

"Some of you are going to need the Family Tree project to make it through science this year." Mr. Wheeler cautioned as he paced in front of Steffie's class. "These last test scores are pretty sorry." He brandished a sheaf of papers at the seated students to make his point.

On shelves near the windows, rows of styrofoam cups held tiny bean sprouts—the latest in the experiments on genetics. "I expect each of you to do a good job on your projects. Be creative. Be original. Make charts. Get photographs. Let's see what went into the making of YOU!" He pointed his finger for emphasis.

"Snips and snails and puppy dog tails!" Herb Gallagher called out.

The class laughed. Mr. Wheeler shook his head in feigned disgust. "I'm grading yours first, Mr. Comedian." Herb groaned. Steffie groaned along with him. Her mind was not on her science project. It was on the man in the white car. She'd looked over her shoulder every step of the way to school. But he had not appeared. Now, she itched for school to be over so that she could walk home with Paul and tell him about it.

For once, neither of them had basketball practice. The All-City Tournament was to begin the next weekend, but Coach Matasik had a meeting on this particular afternoon. Steffie anxiously watched the clock. The hands seemed to creep around the face. When the bell finally did ring, it took fifteen minutes to say good-bye to friends, gather books and adjust sweaters before they were on their way homeward together.

"Did you lose something, Steffie?" Paul asked. "Why do you keep looking around?"

She told him. "You're kidding!" He stopped short after her explanation and stared down at her.

"I'm not kidding! And I'm not making it up. There really was a man in a car watching me. He's been doing it for a long time, too." She tilted her chin in brave defiance, daring him to tease her.

Paul swiveled, scanning the street in all directions. "Well, he's not here now."

It was true. Steffie surveyed the sparse traffic and the parked cars. She didn't see the sedan or the man in the black trench coat. "Well, he was!" she snapped, half-angry that the stranger wasn't sitting there watching for her.

"I didn't say he wasn't." Paul sounded irritated. "Don't be so jumpy." They walked a while in silence. "Did you tell your folks?"

"No."

"Why not?"

She shrugged. "I didn't feel like it."

"Maybe you should," encouraged Paul.

"Maybe I shouldn't." She felt suddenly foolish and stupid. The car wasn't there. The man wasn't there. Paul probably thought she'd made up the whole thing.

"So . . . let's change the subject. How's your Family Tree coming along?"

"Not so good. I think it's a stupid project. And I don't want to do it."

Paul arched his black eyebrows over his chocolate-colored eyes. "You didn't used to think so. What about those old pictures you told me your dad showed you, the ones of your uncle and grandparents? Can't you use them in a photo montage? That's what I'm doing." His easy grin bounced off her dark mood.

Steffie remembered telling him. "They don't show much. I don't think I look like any of them." But the idea appealed to her. A photo montage might look better than an empty tree. At least it might count as "A" for effort.

They were home by now. "Want to shoot some baskets?" Paul asked.

"Not today. I'd better get serious about this project." She didn't want to go inside the big, lonely house. "I'm sorry I got mad about the man in the car."

"It's all right. Maybe the guy is watching you. But one look at me and that might have scared him off."

She smiled and wrinkled her nose. "My hero."

He left her on her front porch and she let

herself in, carefully clicking the lock. The silence overwhelmed her. She didn't want to be alone today.

After getting a snack, Steffie went to her room and spread out her science notes. On green construction paper she drew a tree with branches. The left side, she labeled: "Mother." The right she labeled: "Father." She drew some leaves on each branch and labeled them "Grandparents, Great-Grandparents, Great-Great-Grandparents." The names that she knew, she filled in. She'd get the others from her parents later.

"Why do you always wait until the last minute?" she chided herself. The tree looked skimpy and childish. She tossed it aside and glued together two sheets of yellow construction paper for a photo montage. She remembered that her dad still had the photos. "Terrific!" she mumbled.

On impulse, she decided to find them. Steffie entered her parents' bedroom cautiously, as if they might suddenly appear and ask her what she wanted. The bed was neatly made. Her mother's perfumes, powders, and lipsticks lined her dresser. Her dad's sneakers lay in a heap at the foot of his dresser.

The photo box—where would they keep it?

Steffie wondered. She didn't want to go through their things. But she wanted to find it. She decided to begin in their closet. Opening the door, she found the walk-in closet to be tidy and orderly. Her mom's shoes hung in matched pairs on wire trees. Her father's ties dangled from a special tie rack. The smell of his woodsy aftershave permeated the air.

Nervously, Steffie switched on the light and scanned the overhead shelves. Boxes, bundles of clothes, some old books, and a metal safety box crowded the surface. In one corner, she spied the box marked "Photos." Standing on her tiptoes, Steffie inched it off the shelf. It dropped with a "thunk" into her waiting arms. Anxious to be out of her parents' private room, she carried it down the hall to her bedroom.

There, Steffie settled it onto her bed and pulled back the flaps. Her mouth was dry and she felt as if she were snooping . . . prying, as if she were doing something wrong. "They're my pictures, too!" she said aloud and began to sort through them.

She'd seen most of them before. There were snapshots of her most recent Christmas, her fourteenth birthday, school photos going back for many grades. She recognized several apartment buildings as where they'd lived through the years. She discovered pictures of former friends, long-before Christmases, a few vacations.

"I want the photos of Uncle Charles and Grandma and Grandpa," she said to herself . . . relatives she'd never met. Did they ever think about her? At the very bottom of the box she found a handful of color photos of her dad on the beach with a little girl. His words came back to her . . . *"We've never lived near the sea. Not even when you were a tiny baby."*

Then who was the child? Steffie lay the photos across her bedspread and studied them carefully. Her dad was smiling. He looked much younger. The girl was dressed in a flouncy two-piece swimsuit. She held an over-sized beach ball in pudgy fingers and her potbelly hung over the suit. The child's hair was long and blonde.

Why, it's me! She held the photo up, closer to the light. He had lied to her! They *had* been to the ocean! Cold shudders snaked through Steffie as she gazed at herself in the photographs.

She tossed the pictures aside and searched through the box again. She retrieved more photos of herself. But in the next group, she looked entirely different. She was no more than four years old. And except for the face, she bore no resemblance to the girl in the beach photos. Her long blonde hair had been cropped short. It was a boy's haircut, short and high over the ears, with straight bangs. And in every picture she was dressed in boys' clothing, complete to jeans and polo shirt. She looked exactly like a little boy! A cute, blond, gray-eyed little boy.

Ten

A boy . . . a boy! I look like a boy! Her face gazed outward, childish and innocent from the photo. Her fingers trembled as she stacked the snapshots into a pile. Steffie reclosed the box and returned it to her parents' closet. Her hands did the work. Her mind couldn't absorb what she had discovered.

Back in her room, Steffie restudied the separate groups of photos. The beach pictures were definitely her. She guessed herself to be about three years of age. The other photos showed her looking entirely different at age four. What had happened in that year's time to make her parents cut off her hair and dress her like a boy? she wondered.

Steffie shook her head, trying to clear her mind and remember ten years before. It was no use. Everything was a blank. She couldn't remember. Her earliest recollection was of first grade—Mrs. Snow's classroom, decorated with stenciled streamers of the alphabet.

"What am I going to do now?" She glanced at her alarm clock. Her parents would be home from work in fifteen minutes. At first, she considered running down to them and flinging the photos in their faces. She wanted to yell and scream. She wanted to shout, "Why did you lie to me? Why did you tell me all those fibs? Why?"

But she knew they wouldn't tell her the truth. Why should they? They never had before. She reminded herself defiantly, I have the pictures! She hid them in her drawer, between the pages of her sticker collection notebook. She'd have to think about what to do next. She couldn't decide all at once. She'd have to think of a way to confront them so that they couldn't talk their way out of it.

"Oh, Daddy. . . ." Tears threatened. "Dear, dear Daddy. Why did you do this to me?"

* * * * *

"That game was a real heart-stopper, Steffie! Congratulations!" Steffie's dad looked proudly at his daughter during the ride to the ice cream parlor, following Madison's 42 to 39 win over their rivals.

"Oh, yes, Steffie!" her mom chirped. "What an exciting game! I'm so proud of you . . . the leading scorer!"

Her dad said, "Let's see . . . your team won Friday night, this Saturday morning's game, and tonight's game. That means you'll play in the Finals against Westside next Saturday night. That's the 'Big One'. Think you can take them?"

Steffie was hardly listening. She didn't care about the outcome of the dumb games. She'd played and they'd won, but it hadn't meant anything to her. She certainly didn't care about the championship match in a week.

"I'll treat you to a double-dip chocolate fudge," her father said once they were seated at the ice cream shop. "With whipped cream and a cherry on top like when you were a little girl."

"Was that always my favorite, Daddy?" Her voice contained an edge of sarcasm and she knew it.

"Ever since you were a little tyke." He motioned with his hand to indicate a tiny person no taller than the edge of the table.

"I can't remember that far back. I wish I could."

He held her eyes with his. "You don't seem

nearly as pleased about the game as I thought you'd be, he ventured. "You played so well. Is something bothering you?"

"It was only a game."

"You've been edgy for days, Steffie. Want to talk about it?" her mom asked.

She felt angry words on her tongue. But the ice cream parlor was crowded. She didn't want to create a scene. Besides, she didn't feel ready to ask them about the pictures yet. She shrugged. "No."

Her mom reached over to pat her arm. Steffie withdrew. "I'm going to the restroom." She leaped up from the chair and bolted to the safety of the women's bathroom. She waited for a long time, staring vacantly into the mirror in the neon-lit, white-tiled room. Her feelings churned and bubbled inside her. Abruptly she decided to leave.

Back at the table she licked the cone without much enthusiasm. It tasted thick and cloyingly sweet. It stuck in her throat. Suddenly, she hated chocolate-flavored everything. "I'm full," she said and dumped the cone onto a napkin. Her parents gasped, but Steffie ignored them. Let them wonder! she thought meanly. Let them just wonder!

* * * * *

"That's it? Seven months of talking about it, and that's what you're handing in?" Paul's voice sounded shocked as he held Steffie's construction paper science project in his hands.

They sat on the sofa in Steffie's living room, sipping lemonade and scanning each other's Family Trees. "That's it," Steffie confirmed. By comparison, hers looked pitiful next to Paul's. His tree was bound in a plastic-fronted folder, thick with photos and drawings, and handwritten genealogies.

"Why? I thought you were going to do a photo montage like me."

"I couldn't find any decent photos," Steffie said glumly.

"Mr. Wheeler's not going to be crazy about this."

"Oh, get off my case!" Steffie snapped. "It's just a stupid project and I'm sick of thinking about it. Who cares about 'roots' anyway?" She scowled and snatched the paper from Paul and flopped it onto the coffee table.

"Hey, take it easy. You don't have to chew me up because you're in a lousy mood."

"I'm not in a lousy mood. I just hate all this harping on this stupid project!" Her voice rose in pitch and she felt her anger rise hot and mean.

"Well, excuse me for living!" Paul snapped.

"Well, stop telling me I'm in a bad mood!"

"You live in a bad mood," he retorted.

Steffie sprang to her feet, rage boiling inside her, her fists clenched and her breath coming in gasps. "Why don't you just go away? If I'm so horrible to be around, just go away and leave me alone!"

"I'm on my way, Miss High and Mighty!" Paul jumped up, grabbed his jacket and slammed out the front door. "And walk yourself to school in the morning!" He yelled as he bounded down the porch steps.

Steffie pounded her fists into the sofa cushions, feeling hot tears prick behind her eyes. "I won't cry!" she told herself furiously. "He's a jerk and I won't cry." But it wasn't really Paul she was mad at. It was everything else . . . feelings she couldn't explain, fears she couldn't express.

"Liars!" she said through clenched teeth. Her insides were a seething ocean of anger. "Liars!"

* * * * *

Steffie moped around the house, still in her bathrobe, feeling a little guilty for feigning illness and cutting school. "It's just a cold," she'd told her parents before they left for work. "If I rest today, then I'll be fine. Besides, with the basketball finals Saturday, I want to be sure I'm in top shape."

Her parents had agreed to let her remain home for the day. "I'll call at lunchtime," her mom had said. "Get plenty of rest."

Alone in the house, Steffie shuffled around, snapping the TV off and on, not interested in watching game shows. Her science project was due today. She stared at it for a while, the names of long-dead relatives hung from various leaves. None of the names meant anything to her. Paul had been right. Her project was poorly done. A third grader could have done it better. She tossed it aside, changed into jeans and a long-sleeved shirt, and wandered back downstairs to the living room.

The sun bounced bright and cheerful through the curtains. Suddenly, the house seemed cramped and stuffy to her. On impulse Steffie marched into the hallway, flung open the storm door, and stepped outside onto the porch. She inhaled the crisp spring air deeply, closing her eyes, and filling her lungs. A movement, the sound of a shoe scraping on the bottom porch step, caused Steffie to blink. A short, stocky man in a black trench coat gazed up at her from the stoop.

Too startled to run, too stunned to scream, Steffie only stared at him, open-mouthed. "Don't be frightened, Steffanie," he commanded in a low voice. "I won't hurt you. My name is Phil Korsky and I'm a private detective. Here are my credentials." He reached into his pocket and pulled out a wallet, flipping it open under her nose. She saw an official looking card, showing his picture and the words: "Private Investigator."

"W-What do you want?" Her voice came out in a strangled whisper.

"I've been watching you for months. Making certain you were the girl I'd been hired to find," Mr. Korsky said.

"I-I don't understand." Her legs suddenly went wobbly. Her head felt light, as if she'd run too long without a rest.

His light brown eyes softened and seemed kind. His broad shoulders hunched as he leaned slightly forward, as if to comfort her. "I have someone in my car who wants to see you, Steffanie. Someone who's been searching for you for many years."

"Who?"

"Your mother, Steffanie. Your *real* mother."

Eleven

HIS words crashed against her and Steffie
felt as if all the air had been let out of
her body. She shook her head. "I live with my
mother. . . ." He was mistaken, mixed up.

"Just a minute." The detective turned and
motioned at someone sitting inside a parked
white sedan. A woman emerged. Steffie stared
as she slowly came up the walkway and
stepped onto the porch.

"Sara . . . ," the woman said, her voice
cracking with emotion. She was tall and slim
with short, tossled dark brown hair, a long face
and the darkest of brown eyes, that
shimmered with tears. She reached out.
Steffie recoiled.

"Steffanie," Steffie corrected. "My name is
Steffanie."

The woman shook her head. "It was Sara.
Sara Elizabeth Martin. I named you Sara after
my mother."

"Could we go inside, sit down and talk?" Detective Korsky asked. His tone was kind.

Mutely, Steffie nodded and led the way inside to the living room. *It's a dream*, she thought. *Any minute I'll wake up.* She sat on the edge of the sofa. The woman settled next to her, smoothing the fabric of her beige linen skirt. Phil Korsky perched across from them in her father's recliner.

"I'm Leslie Watson," the brown-eyed woman said. "I was married to Dan Martin fifteen years ago. We had you. When you were two, we got a divorce." She spoke softly, gently, her hands folded tightly in her lap.

"But—but how? Why?" Steffie's mouth was dry. Her question sounded parched, hoarse.

"I know you have a million questions, dear. I'll try to answer all of them. Can I—can I touch you?"

Wide-eyed, numb, Steffie nodded. Tenderly, Mrs. Watson reached out and stroked Steffie's cheek. Her touch was soft. Her fingers trembled. "How much you've grown. . . ." Her eyes brimmed with tears again.

"But my mother . . . "

"Alice is your stepmother." Leslie finished. "She and your father must have married when you were almost four."

"But how . . . ?"

Mrs. Watson's eyes narrowed. "He stole you from me, Sara. Stole you away when you were only three." Her mouth formed a grim line.

Steffie gasped, feeling as if she'd just been slapped. "My father *kidnapped* me?" Her voice now sounded strained and squeaky. "I don't believe you!"

"Tell her all of it, Mrs. Watson," Detective Korsky urged.

Mrs. Watson turned luminous brown eyes onto Steffie. "It was a bitter divorce. We both wanted custody of you, but the judge gave custody to me. Dan had visitation rights, but that wasn't good enough. He swore he'd fight me for you. He hired a lawyer . . . the kind that specializes in parental custody fights. I-I got scared." She shrugged, her shoulders moving in an expensive silk ivory-colored blouse. "I took you away with me."

There was more stunned silence. "You kidnapped me first?"

A wry smile turned up the corners of Leslie Watson's coral mouth. "I ran away with you as far as I could get before I had to take a job and earn enough money to keep on running away. You were such a good little girl!" Her voice rose fiercely. "I would have done anything to keep you, Sara. Anything!"

Steffie's head spun. Her father was

divorced. Alice was her stepmother. Her father was a kidnapper. She didn't believe any of it! Then something bubbled up into her memory. The photos she'd found . . . all the moving through the years . . . the heated arguments between Alice and her father. Like puzzle pieces, the memories began to slip into place and form a picture she couldn't yet comprehend.

"He's robbed me, Sara!" Mrs. Watson cried passionately. "All these years without you. Look at you . . . so grown up. I've been looking for you so long. Tell me you remember something about me. Anything!"

Steffie focused her mind and words came out she didn't even realize she'd spoken. "We played a game. You'd say, 'Hide and don't come out until I tell you.'"

Her mother nodded. "Yes, we lived in motels and moved often. We were always hiding out. Everytime I heard a car drive up, I was certain he'd found us. I made you hide whenever I thought it necessary. We made a game of it."

"In closets, under beds . . . ," Steffie mumbled. "It was always dark. . . ."

"I was so scared," her mother explained. "But one day I got careless. We were sitting out front on the porch of a duplex I'd rented.

You were playing on the lawn. And suddenly, your father drove up, leaped out of the car, snatched you up, and took off. I never saw you again. And I've been looking ever since."

Silence blanketed the room. The ticking hall clock matched the beat of Steffie's heart. She stared at her mother for a long time. The beautiful brown eyes looked back at her, lovingly, longingly. And Steffie believed her.

"Your mother hired me about five years ago." Phil Korsky's voice broke the silence. Steffie turned her head and stared at him. Up close, he didn't frighten her at all. He was just a man with thinning hair and hawkish features. "I had a son who was kidnapped by my ex-wife twenty-five years ago," Mr. Korsky explained. "I haven't seen him since, even though I've been searching all these years." He smiled, as if to himself. "But I was a better detective for Mrs. Watson here." He nodded toward Steffie's mother.

"It's a cruel and terrible thing for one parent to steal a child from another. I've devoted all my professional life to reuniting parents with their kids. I'm glad I found you, Steffie . . . Sara," he corrected. "It makes all the hours of research and legwork worthwhile. Do you understand?"

Steffie nodded slowly. She heard his words,

but the truth still hadn't soaked into her mind. "My Daddy loves me . . . "

"I love you too, Sara!" her mom said heatedly. "And we've so much to make up for . . . so many years lost, wasted."

Steffie blinked back tears and swallowed a lump in her throat. She thought about Alice, now her stepmother.

"Don't go outside without your raincoat, Steffie. You'll catch cold."

"Oh, honey! Did you skin your knee? Poor baby. Sh-sh-sh. Don't cry! Let Mommy kiss it and make it better."

"Steffie, I'm so proud of you! The leading scorer."

"You have a half brother and half sister, Sara." Her mother's voice lured Steffie back into the present.

"I do?"

"I have their pictures." Mrs. Watson fumbled with the clasp on her leather handbag. She withdrew some photos and handed them to Steffie. "This is Matthew. He's ten. And this is Carrie. She's seven."

Child faces grinned back at her. A half brother. A half sister. They had brown eyes. "Do they know about me?"

"Yes, honey. I never stopped thinking about you, talking about you, searching for you. They pray for you every night. They ask about you all the time. We have your photo on the buffet and we talk about how you must have looked as you grew up."

"So I have a stepfather, too?"

"Frank Watson," her mom said. "He's stood by me all these years while I've searched for you. He's paid for everything, because he loves you too, Sara. And you're as much his as Carrie and Matthew. We live in Florida . . . in Melbourne near the ocean. Frank works for an aerospace engineering firm. We've lived in the same house for eight years and we want you with us."

"Selling cars is a great way to make a living. Yes, I know we move often, but I get to meet people and make money at the same time. I'd hate being stuck in an office all day."

"Car salesmen do best in the East and Midwest. No time to loll around on the beach."

"I always wondered what it would be like . . . having brothers and sisters. Paul says it's no big deal . . . "

"Paul?"

"Stupid!" Steffie said to herself. She doesn't know about Paul, or school, or the basketball team, or about my favorite colors. *Daddy! Why? Why?* "Just a friend of mine," she answered.

Her mother reached out again. "May I hug you?"

Steffie shrugged. Why not? Coach Matasik had hugged her once after a big win. "Sure."

Mrs. Watson drew her tenderly into her arms. Steffie tried not to stiffen, but she couldn't help it. She lay her cheek against her mother's soft silk blouse. Her fragrance filled Steffie's senses. She smelled like flowers— roses and jasmine. "Oh, Sara. Dear, dear Sara. I love you so much. I've missed you so much."

Mr. Korsky cleared his throat. With a start Steffie remembered he was still in the room with them. She withdrew from her mother's embrace. "I think we should call your folks," he suggested gently.

"Why?" Mrs. Watson snapped. "I want Sara to come away with me. I want to take her home to Florida right now."

"Now Mrs. Watson, listen to me . . . "

"No! I mean it." Her eyes flashed angrily. "*You* listen! Dan Martin stole her from me eleven years ago. I've missed eleven years out of my daughter's life. I'll never get them back. But I won't allow him to rob me of one more minute. I'm taking Sara home with me. Do you hear? Home, where she belongs!"

She turned to Steffie, her face filled with determination. "Go pack some things, Sara, just a few items, your very favorite things. Don't worry about clothes. I'll buy you all new ones in Florida. Just hurry up. I want you out of this house and away from Dan Martin as quickly as possible. Now, please hurry!"

Twelve

PHIL Korsky rose quickly and put his hand on Mrs. Watson's shoulder. "Please, Mrs. Watson. Sit back down and think for a minute." She obeyed, but Steffie saw the determined set of her jaw. Detective Korsky's voice became gentle as he tried to reason with her. "Think about what's best for Sara . . . running away or talking it out?

"If only you and your ex-husband had talked things out after your divorce, perhaps all this would never have happened," he said. "If you hadn't bolted with Sara, maybe he wouldn't have tracked you and done the same thing. Will taking her away now bring back the past eleven years?"

Mrs. Watson sagged. Steffie felt a strange lethargy steal over her, causing her arms and legs to hang heavy, sluggish, as if they'd gone to sleep.

The detective continued. "You both broke the law, Mrs. Watson. Child-snatching is a crime. If either of you chooses to press charges . . . " He let the sentence trail deliberately, waiting for the implication of his words to sink in. "Is that what you want to do? Press charges against Mr. Martin?" Detective Korsky asked.

Jail! Both her parents could go to jail! Steffie's mind refused to accept this new information.

"No," Leslie said slowly. "No. I don't want to do that. I—I just want to take my daughter home." Her voice cracked and Steffie reached out involuntarily to touch her shoulder. Somehow, it didn't seem as if they were talking about her. Instead, it seemed as if a third person was involved, someone Steffie didn't know.

"Then let me call Mr. and Mrs. Martin now and have them come home. After eleven years it's time you and he faced each other . . . don't you think?"

Mrs. Watson nodded and Steffie watched, detached and fascinated as he picked up the telephone receiver. "Would you give me your father's number at work, Sara?" Detective Korsky asked.

Steffie willed her mouth to form the

numbers, then waited while he dialed. In a few minutes her world would change all over again. Steffie clasped her hands in her lap and counted the squares of bricks in the fireplace. There're so many! she realized. She'd never before noticed how many there were—how many neat little bricks were piled on top of each other to make a fireplace. She sent a sidelong glance toward her mother . . . *Mother. Pretty, brown-eyed, "real" Mother.* Steffie felt tears well as a terrible sense of loss crept over her. *Good-bye, Mom . . . Alice . . . Good-bye . . . .*

* * * * *

It was cold and dark. Steffie shivered, huddled on the cold, hard-packed ground in the cave. Her knees hugged against her chest. Her thoughts sang:

> Three blind mice, three blind mice.
> See how they run.
> See how they run . . . .

Steffie understood why the mice had run. You run when you're scared. You run when you're angry. You run when everybody's tugging at you, begging you to "understand" and "forgive" and saying "I did it for you." You run because it feels good to be free. To have the wind in your hair . . . to be outside and away from people who want to divide you in half.

"We never wanted you to find out like this, Steffie. We wanted to tell you ourselves."

"We love you, Steffie! I've always thought of you as my very own. As if I'd given birth to you myself."

"Sara . . . so much time lost. Come home with me . . . ."

The cave folded her in its dark interior, cool and quiet, shutting out the daylight from the park. The fresh smell of damp earth surrounded her. If I dig straight down, will I come out in China? Steffie wondered, absently digging her finger into the tight, smooth soil.

"I saw the photographs, Daddy. I know we went to the beach when I was little. When did you take me there?"

"After . . . I . . . took you from Leslie. I rented a cottage on the beach in Pensacola, Florida. We lived there for six months. Then I took you to Atlanta."

"I was born in Florida?"

"In Miami where Leslie and I were married, where we divorced."

Steffie sniffed, shivered, and hugged herself more tightly. It was too cold, even in late April, to sit in the cave without a jacket. But she'd forgotten her jacket. She'd just run out the door as fast as she could go, her hands pressed to her ears. No more! She couldn't stand to hear them talking any more—explaining away the past eleven years.

"You cut off my hair. I used to look like a boy. I saw the pictures."

"I thought it would be easier to hide you. No one was searching for a man and his son."

"And Al—Mom?"

"We really were married in Atlanta, Steffie. She's kept my secret all these years. But she's been asking me to tell you the truth for a long time."

Outside the cave, in the park, Steffie knew that it was spring. Lacy fringes of new green adorned the trees. Grass stretched like an emerald carpet. Jonquils, tulips and geraniums lined the footpaths. Toddlers screeched on swing sets and blue skies became a canvas for cotton-white clouds.

Inside the cave, it was dark, cold, and quiet.

"We moved so much because I couldn't let them find us. I knew that if we kept on moving, we'd be harder to trace. We finally bought this house because I was going to tell you the truth. I really was, Steffie."

"You should have told me! You should have told me! All this time . . . all the lies. . . ."

"I love you, honey. Please understand. Forgive me. But I loved you so much. And when Leslie ran off with you, I swore I'd find you and never let her take you away again."

Steffie took a deep shuddering breath. Her shoulder blades ached from hunching. Her eyes burned from dried tears. She pushed a strand of limp hair behind her ear. The quiet in the cave reminded her of holding a sea shell and straining to hear the ocean. All she heard was the "woosh, woosh" of air at the cave's entrance. The ocean inside a sea shell? It was an illusion, a child's game.

"I want you to come back to Florida with me, Sara. Next month you'll be fifteen. I've missed eleven birthdays, Sara. Eleven! It's my turn, Sara. Mine and Frank's and Carrie's and Matthew's."

"They changed my name to Steffanie. I-it's the only name I know. . . . "

"Steffanie, Sara . . . I don't care. Just as long as I can call you daughter."

"You can't take her away."

"You watch me, Dan!"

"Let Steffie decide. You don't want to go away from us, do you honey? This is your home."

"Mr. Martin. Mrs. Watson. Please. This isn't something to dump on the girl right now. You've

*got to work something out. If you two can't . . .
then the courts will."*

The strain across her shoulder muscles stabbed painfully. Steffie flopped back against the hard ground. She stretched her arms over her head and relaxed the muscles, rotating her shoulders in circles. I'm getting dirt smeared into my good yellow shirt. Mom . . . Alice . . . won't like that, she thought.

She heard a rustling at the bushes across the opening of the cave. Slowly, she sat up. She held her breath, cautiously peering into the gloom in front of her. "Go away!" her mind cried. "Leave me alone. Go away!"

The rustling increased. Her heart thudded. *Maybe it's the Big Bad Wolf coming to eat me up.* Yes . . . maybe the wolf will eat me up and I'll never have to go home and face Detective Korsky and Dad and Mother and Alice again, she thought.

Or decide whom I was going to live with . . .

Or have everybody discover the truth about my child-snatching parents . . .

Or become Sara Martin instead of Steffie Martin . . .

Or keep secrets about the past. . . .

Stephanie watched, mesmerized, as the bushes parted.

112

Thirteen

"ARE you in here, Steffie?"

Paul! She slumped as he entered the cave, stooping to avoid hitting his head.

"G-Go a-away."

He lowered himself beside her. "Don't tell me what to do. Your teeth are chattering. Here, take my jacket." He pulled off his letter jacket and slipped it around her shoulders. Instantly, the warmth from his body engulfed her and she clutched the fabric closer. "What are you doing in here anyway? Alone in the dark?"

"Looking for privacy!" she snapped. "I want to be alone."

He looked around the gloomy interior. "It's a good place to be alone all right. No one could find you in here."

"You did."

"I was just guessing." He turned his full

attention onto her. "What's wrong, Steffie? There're two cop cars in front of your house and your parents are calling all your friends, looking for you. They said you ran off about one o'clock. It's after five now. What's going on?"

"None of your b-business." She struggled to control the tremor in her voice.

"I thought we were friends."

"I don't have any friends."

"Everybody was asking about you at school today. I . . . I'm sorry I said those things about your science project. It wasn't so bad you know."

Suddenly she felt light-headed. She felt like giggling. "My science project! Y-you think I'm in here because of m-my stupid science project?"

She saw him stiffen. "Look, I was worried about you. Police don't come out to look for someone unless it's serious."

"You didn't tell them where I was, did you?" She grabbed his arm and glared at him through narrowed eyes. "You better not have."

"Your mom and dad are half-crazy. And who's that other lady? And the man in the trench coat?" He stopped his stream of questions and gaped at Steffie. "He's the man in the white car who's been watching you!

114

That's him, isn't it, Steffie?"

"Yes, that's him!" she sneered. "So what? It's no big deal. Turns out he's a private investigator."

"A detective?" Paul's voice rose in pitch. "Like on TV?"

"Yes, like on TV." She jerked away from the restraining hand he'd placed on her forearm.

"And the woman?"

"My mother."

A long silence fell between them. Paul finally said, "But I thought . . . "

"So did I, Paul." Steffie heard her voice crack as tears brimmed in her eyes. "So did I." She sniffed hard to stem the unwanted flow of tears. Where had they come from? she wondered. She'd thought she was all cried out.

"Are you adopted or something?" Paul asked quietly. "I mean, I've heard about women who give up their babies for adoption, and then years later change their minds. Is that what's happened, Steffie?"

"I'm not adopted." She chewed on her lower lip. "I was stolen." *Stolen! Taken! Seized! Abducted!*

"You mean, like kidnapped?"

"Not exactly." She squirmed against the sudden tightness in her chest. "Do you know what child-snatching is?"

"Why don't you tell me."

She did. She told Paul everything. About her parents' divorce. About her mother stealing her from her dad when she was only two. About the hiding games her mother and she once played. About her dad stealing her from her mother when she was three and of her dad marrying Alice, her stepmother, when she was four. She told Paul and while she told him, she felt as if weights were lifting off of her. *Telling isn't so bad* . . . .

"Wow, what a story, Steffie," he said when she finished talking.

"Sara," she corrected. "My real name is Sara Elizabeth. I was named after my grandmother."

"What are you going to do now?"

"I don't know." Misery settled over her again. "Leslie—Mother—wants me to go away with her. Dad and Alice want me to stay with them. The detective says they can both go to jail because child-napping—even by parents— is against the law."

"Come back with me," Paul pleaded.

"No way."

"What if the police find you and make the decision for you?"

She stared at him in the darkening gloom. "What decision?"

"The decision about whom you go with . . . where you'll stay. Maybe if you come back now, you'll still get a choice about what *you* want to do."

"I-I don't know what I want to do."

"Come back to my house with me," he urged, taking her hand lightly in his. "Let my ma feed you some supper. Let your folks know you're all right. Let the police go away. Then you go to bed and think about it tomorrow."

As if in response to his suggestion of food, Steffie's stomach growled. She released a self-conscious giggle.

Paul punched her arm playfully. "That's more like it. The stomach speaks." She allowed him to pull her to her feet and lead her to the mouth of the cave where he pushed the bushes aside and led her out of the cold, dark interior. She blinked against the offending glare of the dipping afternoon sun. Long shadows formed on the grass, cast by overhead trees.

Paul put his arm around her and turned her toward the pathway home. Step by step, she walked beside him. Her legs felt weak and rubbery. But she leaned against him slightly and let him bolster her. She didn't want to go back to her house. But Paul was right. She had to face them sooner or later.

* * * * *

The had asked her what she wanted to do. Finally, after all these years of deciding for her, now it was her turn to pick and choose. It was her turn to figure out what to do. After all the moving, all the changes, all the lies, Steffie Martin—victim of her parents' private war—had choices. She would make them!

Fourteen

June 15

Dear Paul,

Surprise! Bet you never thought you'd hear from me again. No such luck. It's me! So much has happened since I decided to come back to Florida last April with my mother. I wanted to write you for a long time. But I just didn't until now. Are we still friends?

I've been thinking about everybody back home lately. How's Mickey? And your sisters? And your Mom? My Dad sent me the newspaper clipping about how the team lost the basketball finals to Westside. I'm sorry I ran out on them and Coach Matasik. But I just couldn't stay around for one more minute. Since neither one of my real parents wanted to put the other in jail, the police let us work things out on our own. So—I decided to leave with my mom right away. We had a lot to catch up on.

For a long time, I was angry with Dad and Alice. I was mad at them and wanted to hate them for not telling me the truth. But my feelings are different now. Now I don't hate them any more. I called them for the first time a few nights ago. Dad said how much he missed me, and Alice started crying. So I told them I'd start writing. Being angry won't change anything, will it?

Let me tell you about Florida. We live a block from the beach and I go swimming and surfing every day. At first, Mom wouldn't let me out of her sight. But she's loosened up a lot. I have a gorgeous tan and I've cut my hair short. It's easier to manage now with all the sun and salt-water.

The house here is really neat. It's on one level so I don't have stairs to climb. Mom has wash-and-wear furniture and I have to vacuum every day to get the sand off the tile floors. I have my own room . . . and a brother and sister. (Heavy groan!!!)

You were right about having brothers and sisters. Sometimes they're fun. But they can be a pain, too. Carrie has a lot of silly little friends and she's always into my make-up and jewelry. Matthew can be a real pill. At first they treated me like I was some sort of Queen. But soon the novelty wore off. My stepfather, Frank, is a terrific man. He's been very nice to me and gave up his office at home so I could have my own room and not have to share with Carrie.

I've spent a lot of time with my mother. She's different from Alice. Very busy with church work and stuff. She has her real estate license and sells houses part time. I think she's beautiful and can't figure out why she and Dad divorced in the first place. She doesn't like to talk about the past so I don't ask.

She's showed me dozens of old photo albums and I've talked with my grandparents on the telephone a few times. They live in California so I won't see them until Christmastime when they come to Florida for a visit. It's funny, isn't it? I didn't used to have any house and now I have two. Plus two sets of parents and grandparents and relatives under every rock. Speaking of Family Trees . . . Mr. Wheeler was real nice about giving me a passing grade without turning in my science project. All my teachers let me off the hook. Some let me take a quick final before I left. So anyway, I passed ninth grade.

Well, I guess that's all for now. I need to get to the beach for a couple of runs on my surfboard while the surf's up. Say "Hi" to the gang for me and tell them I miss them all. I'm not sure when I'll ever see any of you again. I guess I'm still mixed up inside about where I really belong.

Your friend,

Steffie

* * * * *

Steffie clutched the telephone receiver, listening to it ring. When someone answered, she felt her mouth go dry. "Hello . . . Paul?"

"This is Paul. Who's . . . Steffie? Is that

you, Steffie?" The phone connection was clear.

She released a self-conscious sigh, suddenly aware that she'd been holding her breath. "It's me."

"Hey! How are you?" It helped to have him so glad to hear from her. "Where are you?"

"Florida." She twirled the phone cord and scuffed the clay-colored vinyl on the kitchen floor. "It's okay. Mother knows I'm calling. She said I could."

A brief, awkward silence fell between them. Paul said, "Thanks for the letters this summer."

"Thanks for writing me back." More silence. "How's everybody?"

"Fine. School starts in two weeks, right after Labor Day. We're all going to Washington High. They have a great basketball team. Tenth grade's going to be different though. I don't even know if I can make the Varsity squad. But I'm going to try. How about you. Does the high school in Melbourne have a good basketball team?"

Steffie noticed that his voice squeeked every now and again. *He's changed* . . . she thought. She moistened her lips. "That's one of the things I wanted to tell you, Paul. I— uh—I'm coming back."

"Hey! That's super!"

His enthusiasm warmed her. She relaxed her grip on the receiver slightly, noticing that her hand had grown sweaty. She wiped it on her jeans and cradled the phone under her chin. "I-I don't want to start all over again in another new school. Mother and Frank are taking it pretty hard. But it's what I want to do."

"Gee, Steffie . . . I guess that was a tough decision. Bet your dad and Alice are glad."

"They're glad. For a while it was like a contest between Dad and Mother about who loved me the most. But not now. They're both my parents. And besides, I miss Dad." Her voice caught and for a minute she thought she might cry.

"The gang will be glad, too," Paul began, talking quickly. It smoothed over the moment. "We'll have a party for you, here at my house!" He paused, adding shyly, "We've-uh-all missed you, Steffie."

Relief flooded through her. She tugged on the phone cord, watching the coil tighten and stretch. "I'll let you know when I'm flying in." Steffie looked up as her mother entered the kitchen. "Look, Paul . . . I've got to go now."

"Sure. Thanks for calling."

"I can still beat you in a game of HORSE."

"Fat chance!"

She hung up and eyed her mother

nervously. "Thanks for letting me call. I hope I didn't talk too long."

"It's all right. You didn't have to hang up. I know how much you miss your friends." Her mother walked stiffly over to the breakfast bar. She clutched her pale-blue satin bathrobe tighter to her body and lowered herself onto a bar stool.

Steffie groped for words, feeling awkward, like something unresolved lay between them. "Mother . . . do you understand why I have to go back?"

"I understand."

"I-I'll be back at Christmas."

"We've already arranged the airline ticket."

"Already?"

"This is Florida, Steffanie. Tourists come to Florida in the winter. And at Christmas . . . " Her voice cracked.

Steffie flew to her arms. "Oh, Mother! Don't . . . "

"You're my daughter. I can't help it. He had you for over eleven years. I've had you only four months. It just isn't fair."

It isn't fair. It isn't fair.

Leslie's arms held Steffie fiercely. "I know it isn't. I love you, Mother." Steffie's voice muffled into the cool satin material. "But I love Dad, too. And . . . Alice . . . ."

She heard the sound of her mother's heart, gentle in her ear. She smelled the faint scent of rose water. Steffie closed her eyes and let the fragrance wrap around her.

Soft . . . sweet . . . Mother smells like roses. A spreading warmth made Steffie feel safe and snuggly.

"I'll be back at Christmas," Steffie repeated. "And then in the summer, I'll come, too. I promise."

Her mother patted Steffie's hair and kissed her forehead. "The past is lost forever, Steffie. I can't ever bring back those years . . . ."

Steffie leaned against her mother for a long time, content to be in her arms. "You'll always be my mother. Always."

"Let Mommy tuck you in, honey. Now give me a kiss. That's my girl! Do you want to know a secret? Daddy and Mommy loves you. More than anything in the whole world . . . we love you best of all."

"Will you always be my Mommy?"

"Of course, I will, honey. Always and forever."

"Contact local authorities if you think you are a victim like Steffie."